Photograph by John Nield

Derek Battle lived in Abertillery for the first fifteen years of life before joining the Royal Air Force. He didn't start writing until his 70th birthday. This, his first novel, was triggered by inactivity in the last period of lockdown.

To. "Mine Hosts"
Matthew and Nicola.
Thankyou for you understanding and support.
I hope you enjoy The Book.

# Angels of the Valleys

Derek Batt

Page 106.

Derek Battle

---

Angels of the Valleys

Vanguard Press

**VANGUARD PAPERBACK**

© Copyright 2024
**Derek Battle**

The right of Derek Battle to be identified as author of
this work has been asserted by him in accordance with the
Copyright, Designs and Patents Act 1988.

**All Rights Reserved**

No reproduction, copy or transmission of this publication
may be made without written permission.
No paragraph of this publication may be reproduced,
copied or transmitted save with the written permission of the
publisher, or in accordance with the provisions
of the Copyright Act 1956 (as amended).

Any person who commits any unauthorised act in relation to
this publication may be liable to criminal
prosecution and civil claims for damages.

A CIP catalogue record for this title is
available from the British Library.

ISBN 978 1 83794 055 4

This is a work of fiction. Names, characters, businesses, places, events and
incidents are either the product of the author's imagination or used in a
fictitious manner. Any resemblance to actual persons, living or dead, or actual
events is purely coincidental.

*Vanguard Press is an imprint of*
*Pegasus Elliot Mackenzie Publishers Ltd.*
www.pegasuspublishers.com

First Published in 2024

**Vanguard Press**
**Sheraton House Castle Park**
**Cambridge England**

Printed & Bound in Great Britain

To my long-suffering wife, Jacky, who supported me
throughout this voyage of discovery.

# Prologue

THE M11 was busy with traffic returning home following the holidays. My daughter, Jo, had packed a small picnic for us in the cool box plus some generous presents were occupying the space between the front and rear seats of our SUV. Despite the volume of traffic, we were making good progress. The holidays seemed to have put everyone in a good frame of mind, and when the VW Beetle with the little dark-haired girl in the back indicated to come out into the fast-lane, I adjusted my speed to create the room he needed to move into. A flash of indicators—truck driver-style—showed his appreciation and the little girl waved through the back window. Judith, my wife, waved back, as did I. The traffic ahead started to slow; brake lights coming on in quick succession. The VW moved slightly to the left of the lane and I chose to favour the barrier side of the lane. Both the VW and I had slowed to a walking pace when I first became concerned with a coach in the fast lane behind me. Approaching much too fast, it was obvious to me and the front seat passengers in the coach that they were going to crash into us. Much too late, the coach driver raised his head and realised his and our predicament. The coach, its brakes locking all wheels, slammed into the back of us. My SUV, with the brakes off as I tried to find some safe space, shot forward. The front wheels riding up the sloping back of the Beetle sent my SUV skyward. I mashed down on the brake pedal—to no avail, we were airborne. The twisting motion imparted by the rounded shape of the VW threw my car into a spin. The SUV cleared the central barrier in a perfect barrel-roll. The rate of roll was perfect. The SUV landed, squarely, on all four tyres. Could we escape the crash? Just as that thought arrived, so did the Mercedes Sprinter. It hit the passenger door, sending us spinning into the centre lane and the path of the Toyota. From safety to destruction was milliseconds. The screeching of tyres and the tearing of metal was horrendous, compounded by the sounds of blaring horns from cars and lorries signalling that they knew they were about to crash but could do nothing to prevent it. The noise suddenly ceased and other senses took over, checking for the smell of fuel and the approach of rescue. My injuries finally robbed me of consciousness. The silence was deafening and the darkness total…

# Chapter 1

T̲HE̲ universe was spinning, the stars and planets revolving around a rainbow "red and yellow and pink and green, orange and purple and blue." The rainbow faded and the large yellow planet with a white glowing atmosphere swung into view. The centre of the planet split and a violent yellow and green torrent spewed forth. The oxygen mask clamped tightly to my face as the steam catapult threw the F14 down the deck of the carrier. "Highway to the Danger Zone" echoed in my headset as the WOG switches triggered the undercarriage to retract. From the edge of consciousness, Major Tom asked whose shirt I wore and I zoomed away towards the black hole at the centre of my being. Just before the event horizon, a refuelling hose extended towards me and a quiet voice said, 'the Valium should calm him down.' As I slipped into the ever-darkening tunnel, a siren sang. A large white owl in horn-rimmed glasses gave his team some wise words and the cool rush of drugs sent me spiralling into a deep coma…

My arms ached as I was pulled from the depths, my head seemed to clang with each rung of an imaginary ladder and the light at the surface slowly increased in intensity. People were talking, to me, at me or to encourage me to wake up. The comfort of sleep was too much and I descended back to the warmth with American Pie being sung tunelessly from above.

I finally woke at night with the singing nurse, Mikela, moistening my lips. I don't know who was the most surprised. Clarity arrived slowly. I realised the rainbow could have been the bruise along my right thigh and the big yellow planet had, in fact, been the sick-bag that Mikela said I filled on many occasions.

Morning rounds started with me, the star patient. The doctor, the owl of my dreams, read my notes and welcomed me back to the land of the living. I asked about my prognosis and got the standard answer, 'if you can pass water and open your bowels, we can consider sending you home.' As for my injuries, there was bruising externally but the main problem had been bruising internally to my liver, spleen and stomach. The slight internal bleeding had been stemmed by drugs so no surgery had been needed. I asked about my wife and immediately knew the answer. The doctor confirmed she had been pronounced dead at the scene. For the next two days, I worked hard to open my bowels, but where I had been, no toilet had been necessary and my body seemed reluctant to give up anything. I was allowed to walk around the ward and even take a shower. I intentionally stuffed myself with any food or sweets I could get hold of. Finally, on the evening of the third day my bowels opened.

My daughter, Jo, having been told of the change in my condition, had travelled from her home to the hospital which was just outside Cambridge to visit me in the afternoon. It was a strange, and for her, difficult visit. I was alive and seemed to have recovered from all injuries. My wife, her mother, on the other hand, had passed away. She told me how she had driven up to Norfolk, and after talking with my neighbours, had employed a lady to keep the place tidy. From a book that my wife and I had put together, she arranged her mother's funeral and the interment in the Buxton Church cemetery. She produced a book to show the bills to be paid and people to be thanked in person, by phone or in writing. Having completed my ablution tasks the doctor decided I could go home. Jo drove me back to Norfolk. The house was strangely quiet so we decided to go to a local pub for an evening meal. We talked a lot but said little, and after a further glass of wine at home, we decided to call it a night. Jo left early the next morning. I spent the morning ringing friends and relatives that had made the effort to give Judith a good send-off. I also travelled around to local providers to pay for the funeral, flowers and catering. The vicar, who we also knew as chairman of the parish council, was very kind and said she was very glad to see such a large turnout. We exchanged pleasantries for a few minutes more and I took my leave.

I slept for an hour and then made myself a sandwich for lunch. The pain in my thigh and hips was pretty intense and I decided to take some painkillers washed down with a vodka. The second vodka killed the pain and I slept for three hours. I took a call from Jo and assured her things were all good. We talked about the accident and whether the insurance company had been informed. She confirmed that she had spoken to the police but no resolution had been reached. My day ended with painkillers and more vodka.

My head throbbed as I waited for the coffee to percolate. Today, I needed to speak to the insurance company and brief a solicitor if necessary. I also needed to visit the surgery, hopefully, to get some painkillers and be referred to a physiotherapist. The doctor prescribed the painkillers but there was no physio time available. He did, however, get me six sessions with a personal trainer at the local sports centre, of which I was already a member. My call to the insurance company was very much easier than I could have hoped for. We agreed I did not need a replacement car and a payment of 1.2 million pounds would not make up for the loss of my wife but would ease the pain for myself, Jo and the grandchildren. For the next two weeks, my personal trainer, Jamie, put me through a not-too-strenuous series of stretches and exercises. By the time my NHS sessions had finished, I was in a much better state of health. I booked further sessions with Jamie to improve my strength and stamina and began swinging the golf clubs again at my club's practice ground.

The blackness began to close in after a few weeks. Loneliness is a terrible thing and always seems to visit just when you seem to be getting over the loss of a loved one. My problems were not only missing my wife but I also started getting a vision of old friends from my school days. I could not get thoughts of Terry and Sheila out of my mind. Terry was probably my oldest friend, we went right back to primary school. Terry and Sheila had been friends since grammar school, and I assumed, had become an item after I left for the Air Force. I say visions because I was something of a psychic. The previous year, I had assisted the Norfolk police in the search for a missing girl. We did find her but not alive.

The phone call came out of the blue from Detective Inspector Ian Forbes from Abertillery Police station. He apologised for calling without warning or introduction but had been given my details by a reporter with the Eastern Daily Press. There was a young girl missing in the local area and the family were suggesting that the use of a psychic could bring some clues that the police seemed unable to find. Ian Forbes had asked some local ladies who had reputations as white witches but they declined, saying they had no experience in the field. They had, however, heard of a man in Norfolk—me. Ian also mentioned that the Western Mail had put up a £25,000 reward. I enquired as to a good hotel and contact details for the white witches. The call really raised my spirits. I packed my case and my golf clubs and loaded them into the car. I contacted the lady who had kept house whilst I was in hospital and agreed a price to look after the house again. Andy, my neighbour, agreed to look after my garden. I went to bed early and set the clock for two-thirty a.m. Leaving at three-fifteen a.m., I drove steadily for six hours, stopping once for the toilet at an M4 service station. By midday, I had arrived at a nice-looking hotel overlooking the reservoir at Cwmtillery. The receptionist gave me the price for a junior suite with a deck overlooking the lake and we agreed I could have it for a month.

I phoned the white witches and invited them for coffee. Due to their daily schedules, they could not meet me until after lunch so we arranged for a meeting at one-thirty p.m. I decided to drive around the town. I had lived in this town for fifteen years but had not been back for thirty-five years. The town had changed, but after a few minutes of driving around, I was able to orientate myself and the place became more familiar to me.

I have preconceived ideas about most things and white witches should be goths dressed in black with tattoos and coloured hair. The two young ladies who met me in the hotel looked like schoolteachers, in fact, they were both married with young families. After our initial introductions, we considered whether we should get involved in the case and how long we should spend on it if we were not successful. The girls agreed to take part but would only be available during school hours. The promise of a reward sweetened the deal but the terms still needed to be confirmed. In the course of conversation, I mentioned my friends, Terry and Sheila, and after several questions, Megan said she knew Sheila and would contact her to see if they wanted to meet up.

We started a TO-DO list;

    1. Contact the family
    2. Talk with the Western Mail regarding the rewards.
    3. Meet with Ian Forbes as to how we would be received by the local police.
    4. Try to get a copy of the police file or create a file from press coverage.

I also questioned the girls on their psychic experience and which specialisation, if any, they preferred. Megan was a seer and used meditation to receive comments and directions. Gwyneth too was a seer but was adept with dowsing rods and could focus the rods depending on what she was searching for. Before she left, Megan rang the Merediths and arranged a meeting for tomorrow morning at the hotel. I rang the Western Mail and was put through to Harry Blackmore who agreed to meet us after lunch tomorrow. He said any reward would be dependent on our story being published in his paper, thereby offsetting the cost of £25k. Ian Forbes answered his phone in his official voice and agreed we should meet soonest. Fifteen minutes later, he was sitting in the bar of my hotel with a pint of bitter in a straight glass. His first mouthful emptied half the glass. I arranged coffee for the ladies and myself and we introduced ourselves. Ian was 'old school,' standing close to six foot with a build of a second-row forward, which he was and had, only recently, hung up his boots. He was vocal in his opposition to the lowering of the height limit for policemen and had little regard for policewomen. Ian refilled his glass and I began to wonder if we were to be welcomed or if this was going to be a hands-off warning. As it turned out, we were welcomed with only a slight warning. Ian would not countenance any interference with his investigation. However, he had a copy of the official file of the Claire Meredith case which he would leave with us. He felt for the family and admitted that the police had, so far, drawn a blank. He knew of our backgrounds and understood why the family had sought an alternative solution. He knew our motives were altruistic and reward-driven. He asked that his office be kept abreast of any progress and named Sergeant Dave Williams as our official liaison. He took his leave and left the manila envelope on the table; Dave Williams's business card was stapled to it. The file was a photocopy of the official file. We read the file and soon realised that there was little of any consequence in it. No wonder the police had made no progress. There was NO EVIDENCE. I spent the next hour swimming gently in the local sports hall pool. Swimming allowed me to review all the information we had collected. As I digested the information of the last three days, I was also able to consider the changes in my personal life. I had lost my wife and been given a large sum of money and was now back in my town of origin. I arrived at my hotel shortly after five p.m. and sat in the bar with a beer. I already had several scenes in my head. The empty street was bathed in light from the street lamps. A vehicle, barely visible from my viewpoint, with no make or registration evident. Most remarkable and disturbing was a large black pyramid. The next morning, I returned to the sports hall for a pre-arranged session with a personal trainer. Arwell listened to my requirements and quickly devised a programme to stretch out every muscle in my body. After forty-minutes minutes of torture, I returned to the hotel, showered and went down to breakfast. Megan turned up early and ordered coffee on my breakfast menu. She appeared to be in a mischievous mood and took several minutes to pump me regarding my growing up in Abertillery. I explained that I was born in Abertillery and went to the grammar school until 1966 when I joined the Royal Air Force. She continued to ask about my early love life and I started to get defensive. She then explained her mother had known a boy with the same name as me and he had joined the RAF in 1966.

She was Susan's daughter!

I would have loved to pursue the matter but Gwyneth had arrived and we needed to get on with the day's work. I had rearranged the sitting room as an office to allow the three desks provided by the hotel to be placed back-to-back. Large-scale maps of Abertillery and one of South Wales were folded to allow the immediate area to be displayed. We sat around a smaller round table to discuss the previous day and any thoughts from our individual consultations. The two girls had a good giggle that I knew Megan's mother, but we soon settled down and began our first recorded session.

*I went first and recounted;*
*the darkening street with the lights coming on,*
*a vehicle of unknown type,*
*and a large black pyramid.*
*Gwyneth went next;*
*she saw a doctor in a white coat.*
*Megan came last;*
*she saw a tennis court,*
*And a wide, open field.*

We talked through what we had seen but no idea came immediately to mind. The human mind is simple and started its search for a matching area close to the snatch site in Carlisle Street and then moved slowly outwards in concentric circles. From the circles, we searched areas known to us as individuals. As psychics, we try to absorb and select energies from the environment. Nothing manifested itself. Gwyneth wrote our comments on the whiteboard. We stopped for the ladies to do the school run.

The afternoon found us around the table reading Claire's file.

The file was thin and separated into three sections.

Section 1. A description of the family, including the missing girl and a description of the immediate area.

Section 2. Several witness statements from people who saw nothing, heard nothing and knew nothing.

Section 3. A short timeline from the time Claire went missing to the present.

We sat around the desks that the hotel had provided for a small fee and read and reread the file. Megan made comments on the first of the whiteboards the hotel had also supplied. We spread a large-scale map of the area around Abertillery on the desks and took a few moments to concentrate on Carlisle Street. Whilst we felt that something had happened, we were only able to feel a slightly-raised temperature. The ladies had to go to do the school run and we agreed to do individual research overnight and meet with the Merediths in the morning.

The Merediths, Martin and Julia, were early. By ten o'clock, we had coffees in front of us and had made the initial introductions. They were both young, twenty-seven, and Claire was their only child. Megan had positioned the voice recorder, and after gaining their permission to record the interview, we gently probed for the information that would build a picture for us to tease out the facts.

Me. 'Tell me about Claire.'

Martin. 'She is a normal seven-year-old, cheeky, full of energy, loved playing with her friends. She was very happy at school and loved music.'

Julia. 'She loved animals especially cats.'

Me. 'What was her normal bedtime and her home time?'

Julia. 'It was school holidays so we let her play out till nearly dark. On school nights she had to be in by six-thirty p.m.'

Megan. 'On the day she went missing, what time did you miss her?'

Martin. 'I went to look for her at seven o'clock.'

Gwyneth. 'What time did you last see her?'

Julia. 'Just after five o'clock, she came in for the toilet.'

Gwyneth. 'Were you both in all afternoon?'

Julia. 'Yes, Martin got home from work about two-thirty p.m. and we were together until Martin went to look for Claire.'

Me. 'Did Claire and her friends go near the rivers?'

Julia. 'No, all the children are told to keep away.'

Me. 'What kind of things did Claire like?'

Julia. 'Like what?'

Me. 'Sweets, cakes, ice cream, chocolate, kittens, anything.'

Julia. 'Why?'

Me. 'If she was taken, she may have been enticed into a vehicle. Do you give her the normal warnings of sweets from strangers and strange vehicles?'

Julia. 'Yes, all the time. She did like small animals.'

Megan. 'Who was she playing with when she went missing?'

Julia. 'Her best friends, Mary and Joan Mason, at number twenty-one.'

Megan. 'Do you know what time they went in?'

Julia. 'Six-forty-five p.m., according to their mam.'

Me. 'So, Claire was alone after six-forty-five p.m. Did she enjoy playing on her own, some children do?'

Martin. 'Sometimes, especially hopscotch, but normally closer to our front door.'

Me. 'Are you both aware that the chances of finding a person alive after forty-eight hours are very small?'

Martin and Julia. 'Yes.'

Me. 'The family has put up a large reward and may not receive a good outcome.'

Martin. 'We want her alive, but if it's not possible, we need to give her a proper send-off.'

The interview reinforced the impression that I had already formed from the file interviews of friends, family and neighbours, that the family were not involved in the disappearance.

We promised the Merediths we would do our best to find their daughter, and after a tearful farewell, settled in to review the interview tape.

After lunch, we took a quick trip to Carlisle street. I knew the area well, having been bought up in Glan Ebbw Terrace. There was very little, if any, information to be gleaned from a three-week-old, crime scene. We decided to take the rest of the day off and give the case some individual thought.

We reconvened at nine-thirty a.m. the next day. I had unpacked my inert earth crystal pendant and tripod. The inert earth crystal pendant is a rose gold cage about sixty-seven millimetres long and about twelve millimetres in diameter. At the one end of the hollow cylinder, is a point made of inert earth crystal, the other end is flat with a swivel attached to a gold chain. Inside the cylinder are alternate discs of gold and aluminium. The tripod is aluminium with a roller ball on the end of each leg. When suspended above a map, a seer or seers can activate the crystal, allowing it to swing within the tripod, and thereby, move it to an area sought by the seer. We sat around the table and tried to channel our energies through the crystal pendant to where Claire or her body was. Our energies slowly started the pendant to swing. The momentum of the pendant is small, and it moves exceedingly slowly. Another idiosyncrasy of the crystal, was its ability to store energy and continue to track a location without the seer's presence. We broke for lunch with the unit slowly tacking a distant target. When the ladies returned from lunch, the pendant had stopped over a target that explained all of the items that we had SEEN. We repositioned the unit from a different starting point and concentrated until we were sure the tripod was moving. After three attempts, we were certain we had identified our target. Having a clear understanding of the site, it was more likely than not to be a grave. I phoned the number for Dave Williams but he was out. The operator volunteered to have him call me back. As the ladies left for the day the phone rang. Dave Williams introduced himself and I told him who I was and what I believed we had found. He was in his car coming back from Brynmawr and would drop in for a drink if it was convenient. I agreed and arranged to meet him in the bar. No sooner had I ordered and walked to a very quiet table than he walked in. In a suit, decent shoes, polished, and a tie picked by his daughter, as it turned out. One hundred-and-seventy-five centimetres and still a figure like a racing snake. He was a rugby player of much repute who still turned out every Saturday, if only for the seconds. We seemed to hit it off from the start. His afternoon at Brynmawr had been on the golf course. When we were settled, he got back on the subject of Claire Meredith. I quickly brought him up to speed and explained we could not be certain until we walked the area and dug for the grave. He was ambivalent about psychics but didn't want to call in the cavalry in case we were wrong. I gave him the location and said we would be there by ten o'clock.

The ladies arrived just after nine a.m. in working gear. Gwyneth carried a set of dowsing rods and we borrowed three shovels from the hotel. We decided to take two cars and leave one a short way from the actual site. The site was on the north side of Abertillery Park. As we approached the park from Glandawr Street, we started to see the items that had appeared during our sessions. The tennis courts adjacent to the park cottages and the open field, which was known locally as the "extension," at the end of which stood the black pyramid. The pyramid was the spoil tip from the Roseheyworth Colliery. We dropped Gwyneth's car close to the tennis courts and the three of us went forward in mine. There was a path running around the western circumference of the tip. We parked about fifteen metres away and started towards the tip as Dave Williams drove up. He parked alongside us and was obviously happy with our initial attempts to preserve the site. I introduced him to the ladies and then we moved onto the path which was seven or eight metres above the Ebbw River. We walked slowly in single file with Gwyneth leading. We were looking for any signs of disturbance. We reached the far end of the spoil pile without detecting anything. Slightly dejected, we turned around and began walking back, this time Gwyneth, still leading, produced her dowsing rods. The rods initially twitched towards the river, but using her energy, the rods became parallel and pointed straight ahead. The base of the tip was shaped like several peanut shells having cut-outs every fifty metres or so. As we passed the second to last indent, the rods flickered to the left towards the tip, and as Gwyneth took her next step, both rods swung hard-left, a sure indication of something. Looking closer, we were able to see an area of disturbance that had been replaced with care and the spoil, with a covering of grass, had been replaced almost perfectly. The recent rain had tamped the area down and running water had outlined the area. Dave Williams and I started to dig the area. Within forty-five centimetres, we uncovered a black industrial-strength plastic bag closed with a yellow zip-tie. Dave manipulated the bag and convinced himself that it was a small body. Removing a pen knife of almost legal length from his pocket, he inserted the tip into the plastic bag, and with what could be described as an evil hiss, the bag was slit open. Inside the plastic bag was a plastic sheet that you put on a child's bed against toilet accidents. The knife slit the sheet and the nylon or rayon sheet below that. The tiny face was grey and relaxed, with eyes closed against the pain she had obviously endured and the sights she had seen. A serrated knife had left a jagged tear where her throat should have been. Dave looked up and swallowed several times before his training kicked in and he became Sergeant Williams. He asked us all to leave and take only what we had bought to the site. From his car, he collected stakes and police tape to preserve the site. Several phone calls and a radio call and the cavalry were on the way.

As the different sections arrived, we became less and less involved. We moved back to my car and waited. Thirty minutes later, Dave came over to us and asked that we leave and return to the hotel, where both Ian Forbes and the Chief Constable of South Wales, Lionel Jeffries, were waiting for us.

We dropped Gwyneth at her car and made our way down the narrow road to join Glandawr Street just beyond the Red Ash. Megan quietly said she had spoken to her mother the previous evening and she had asked after me. If I wanted, she would like to meet for a drink sometime. We weren't sure what the next three or four days would involve and meeting Susan would be a pleasant aside. Was she married? She has been divorced for the past seven years. Megan passed me a business card with Susan's contact details on it.

The hotel bar was as crowded as I had seen it. Several people were, what I would have called, 'brass' but on the police uniform was silver braid. Ian Forbes intercepted us and took our drinks order. He then introduced Chief Inspector Lionel Jeffries. Lionel was just about tall enough to have scraped into the police when they had a height restriction. However, it was his girth that surprised me. He was built like one of the Pontypool front-row, which, I was to learn, he could well have been. He had been first reserve, front-row forward for that formidable unit. Once you absorbed his size and the facts of his rugby history, it was his eyes that took your attention. They were blue and never still—they reflected his razor-sharp mind and a pleasant sense of humour. As Ian handed out the drinks, Lionel proposed a toast on our success in the Meredith case. We accepted the accolade with good grace, but I had a nagging feeling we had only scratched the surface of this case. The black pyramid flashed into my mind as if we had unfinished business. Dave turned up to report that the body had been removed to the morgue and the site had been cleared forensically. Two bobbies in shifts would protect the site until the autopsy had been completed. With Dave and Ian chatting with the ladies, Lionel took me to one side. He understood that we had been invited to work the case by the family and that we were attracted by the reward. However, his officers had worked this case for nearly four weeks without any prospect of the reward. I agreed with his sentiments and asked if he had any idea how we could give something to the rank and file. He asked if we could make a contribution to the Police Welfare Fund. I liked the idea and said I would put it to the ladies, and if they agreed, we would make the fund an equal partner in any rewards. Overjoyed, he shook my hand and we rejoined the throng. The ladies were driving and had to leave for the school run. Megan gave me the thumb and little finger shake reminding me to phone

Susan. Dave tapped me on the shoulder and handed me a pint of bitter. He asked me to come and meet someone who I had only spoken with previously. We moved to a booth near the window overlooking the reservoir. Sitting across the table was a rotund individual who had spent a lot of his life sitting and sipping his favourite tipple, Bell's whisky. He was dressed in suit trousers with a short-sleeved shirt closed with a florid yellow tie and matching braces. His name was Harry Blackmore. He would become very well-known to me and the ladies, as he was our access to the reward offered by his paper the Western Mail. He would also be instrumental in embroiling us in the cases of Missing Angels. We talked for a short time and he explained that access to the reward for the Meredith case would be subject to the three of us being interviewed by him to be published in the Mail. By the time he left, Dave and I were the only ones in the bar. Dave then excused himself and invited me to the post-mortem if I liked, ten-thirty at the morgue. Beer or bravado, I agreed. I went up to my room and tidied it up a bit. I made a coffee and sat on the balcony looking out over the lake. My phone rang just before seven. It was Susan. The voice I had last heard on 30$^{th}$ August 1966, the day before I left for the Air Force, sounded apprehensive and frail. She phrased her questions carefully as if worried about the replies. After the first two minutes, it was as if we had never been apart. I explained how the afternoon had gone and I would not be able to pick her up, but I would like to invite her to the hotel for dinner. She accepted and said she would drive over.

Susan arrived before eight; time had been very kind to her. She had chosen blue Levi's, a pale lemon blouse and a black V-necked jumper. Her shoes were sensible; black court shoes with a small heel. At her throat was a fine gold chain and the choice was echoed on her left wrist and in slight drop earrings. Her hair was still black and worn at shoulder-length. Everything about her whispered class but the only outward show of money was a stainless-steel ladies' Rolex. She chose coffee and we settled on a table close to the television in case the conversation became stilted. It didn't; we asked the polite questions and then reminisced right back to August 1966. A light meal of fish, washed down with a lovely white wine saw eleven-thirty come around much too quickly. I walked her to her car. She slipped her arm through mine as we left the hotel door. At her car, she said it was lovely to see me. I asked if she wanted to do it again tomorrow as I had arranged to dine with Terry and Sheila, my best friend from school and her niece. She agreed.

The day had been emotional and very long, and coupled with a fair consumption of alcohol, sleep came quickly. My dreams were returning to the black pyramid when the room phone interrupted. It was Sergeant Dave Williams, the post-mortem was delayed to two o'clock and he would like to arrange for the three of us to be interviewed following the finding of the body. I looked at the clock, seven-thirty a.m. I swore down the phone but soon started laughing as I heard him chuckle. He agreed to ten o'clock. A swim, a shower and a fried breakfast saw me arrive by taxi at the police station just before ten. The ladies were already there and Megan gave me a knowing look. 'You have spoken with your mum, then.' To which she smiled and said that she really enjoyed it. Did I blush? We were separated and taken to individual interview suites. We were read our rights and it was explained that, because of our unusual involvement, our interviews would be conducted under oath and become part of the case file. A sergeant with a police constable in attendance conducted the interview in accordance with police procedure. It took the best part of an hour. The tapes, two of them, were sealed and I was asked to sign and date both. The second copy was labelled and given to me and the other was signed into evidence.

All three interviews finished at about the same time. The ladies had to collect their children and they declined the invitation to the post mortem. Before they left, Gwyneth said she felt we had unfinished business with the black pyramid. She explained that both she and Megan had dreams of the tip. I was busy in the afternoon so asked the girls to meet at nine o'clock tomorrow.

## Chapter 2

THE post-mortem examination is normally carried out to ascertain the cause of death or to provide evidence and information to identify the deceased. In this case, the cause of death was obvious and the identification could have been left to the parents. The purpose of this post-mortem was to gather evidence against the person or persons who had abused and killed a beautiful angel.

Professor Gwynfor Davies cleared his throat and began a commentary that would last thirty-five minutes. He moved with a practised ease which belied his sixty-seven years. The body was examined in detail. Each nick and blemish was noted and the assistant stepped in to take photographs as he was instructed to do so. The head and torso were opened and every organ was examined for damage. The brain and liver were weighed. Samples of fluids were taken measured and labelled. When he was finished, Gwynfor closed the microphone and instructed his assistant to close. He met us in the outer lab, and seeing Dave, he announced, "not a nice one, Dave". Dave asked for a cause of death and Gwynfor replied, "lacerations to the throat with a heavily-serrated weapon. The body had been vaginally and anally abused in a violent manner, causing tearing to both orifices. She did not have a pleasant death. My report will be with you by five o'clock tonight."

We shrank away from the morgue and found refuge in the Conservative Club. It was impossible to unsee that small body lying on the stainless-steel table but we hoped a few beers would help. As the crowd went back to work or home, I sat with Dave and asked if Claire was the only young girl to have gone missing lately. He looked slightly shocked or embarrassed; it was difficult to tell. 'Why did I ask?' I explained that Megan, Gwyneth and I were still getting visions of the tip. This could indicate that we had missed further targets and the energy of Claire's remains may have masked others in the area. The longer they were in the ground, the less energy we were able to pinpoint. Dave had to go but he told me to ask Harry Blackmore who he said was always talking of a serial killer. I walked back to the hotel. The two miles seemed more like ten. With an hour or two to spare, I went to the hotel pool. It was small but I am no Olympic swimmer. I showered and dressed, noting that I needed to put some laundry in or buy some new clothes. I was still early so I did put a load of laundry into the hotel system.

Sheila was the mother of three children and was very comfortable with her lot. She had always been cuddly but attractive to the boys in our group. Terry had lost his mop of unruly black hair that had been his most instantly recognisable feature but was still the man that had been my best friend from infants through to the grammar school fourth year when I had taken my leave. Tony had followed his dad into the family building business and played guitar with several local groups. We managed to get the table by the window overlooking the lake. The table was laid for four, which drew comment from Sheila. I said we had another guest arriving shortly and she gave me a knowing look. We took the menus and ordered pre-dinner drinks. Susan joined us much to the amusement of Sheila. Sheila was instrumental in putting her aunt and a rather shy friend, (me), together back in 1966. Susan had made a great effort; new hair-do, a plain dark-blue shift dress with matching shoes and black tights. The same plain bracelet and earrings complimented, with a slightly heavier chain at her throat and a gold watch.

It turned out Sheila had an almost total recall and kept us entertained with our exploits from forty years previously. Like myself, they married young but did manage to get to go to university before they tied the knot. They asked about my service career which I was only too willing to recount with embellishments. I was more reluctant to talk about my wife but Susan supported me as the details were coaxed from me. The dinner was a great success and Terry and Sheila left just after eleven. They only lived about half a mile away and chose to walk home. I asked Susan if she wanted coffee and she answered, "shall we take them up?"

# Chapter 3

THE interviews with Harry Blackmore were very interesting. He delved deeply into our pasts, probing gently with intelligent questions. Unlike most people, Harry seemed to accept that gifted people were real and he even acknowledged that members of his own family "saw things." Gwyneth left just before lunch to collect her youngest from school. We ordered a lunchtime drink, Harry was a Bell's man even at midday. We were all finished by three-thirty and Harry produced a cheque for the reward made out to me. I accepted with good grace. I broached the subject of other young girls having gone missing. Harry took a swig from his drink before he answered. The figure startled me. There were approximately thirty young girls that had gone missing over nearly twenty years. He produced a neat file about five centimetres thick. He passed it across to me.

"That is for you, if you decide to look into these missing persons cases. If you do start to look at these cases, your perception of the South Wales police will diminish. The level of co-operation you receive will reduce to zero. If I am correct in the assumptions I have drawn, the police have been so fragmented that they have completely missed the operation of a monster. The police seemed incapable of inter-valley communication. The valleys and the corresponding mountains seemed to channel messages north and south but prevented east/west communication. The early radios had insufficient range and telephones were limited, with too many switchboards. Even when equipment improved, the police procedures and hidebound opinions of its officers prevented the sharing of information." Astounded, I accepted the file, and with it, the task of investigating a serial killer.

Megan then gave me twenty minutes of, "what are your intentions towards my mother?" She did admit that her mum was very happy to have met up with me again and did seem to have a spring in her step. I replied that I was going to stay around for as long as I felt wanted. I had no intention of marrying again. Susan had invited me for dinner and provided a good wholesome meal of steak and onions with a light mash and green vegetables. I was pre-occupied with the Blackmore file and left early, being back in my room before eleven. I placed my favourite tipple close at hand with the ice bucket and the file. I filled the glass with vodka and coke, took a swallow and added the ice. I opened the file with some trepidation. The file was divided into thirty cases in chronological order, with Claire Meredith on top, the first case in the file. I read the file for a couple of hours. Once I became familiar with the layout, it was easy to extract information. Harry had tabulated the cases with date, name of victim, age, place from which missing, police jurisdiction and found/not found. Each case was **not found.**

I was a little jaded when I went down to breakfast. What I had gleaned from a couple of hours of reading was causing me a great deal of concern. The ladies arrived just after the school run and came dressed for an expedition. We sat around the table and wondered why we kept returning to the black pyramid. Gwyneth wanted to go back and walk the ground again. Megan wanted to call the police in and let them do the donkey work. I relayed my meeting with Harry and what I had learned from Harry's file. If he was right, we would be searching for thirty victims of a serial killer. I believed we had missed targets in the tip and we were being called back to trace them. We had already earned £25,000 reward by the Western Mail for Claire. If there were further targets, we should be the ones to indicate their presence, and therefore, claim any further rewards. The ladies agreed. After making enquiries with the hotel front desk, I had a contact number for the local detectorist club. John Evans was a retired teacher who took up detecting for fitness and fun. He was available this morning but was very suspicious of our targets and our motives. The offer to pay his expenses in cash seemed to encourage him and he said he would meet us there by eleven a.m.

At the tip, Gwyneth walked the path with Megan three metres behind her. They walked very slowly along the path from south to north. About one hundred-and-fifty-metres up the path, the dowsing rods twitched slightly and

Gwyneth asked Megan to mark it. This process was repeated once more before the path petered out. Gwyneth was deep in thought as she scanned the face of the tip. She walked further around the northern extreme of the tip and her face lit up. Another path was evident about fifteen-metres above the lower one. She scrambled up to the higher path, and dowsing slowly, walked the path from north to south. Megan placed two more red flags along the uphill side of the path. John Evans, as good as his word, turned up as Gwyneth returned to the car with an excited glow in her eyes. John assembled his eighteen-inch detector as I instructed him on the area to be searched and that any target would be only forty-five-centimetres down. Within forty minutes, John had covered the designated area twice and confirmed the presence of anomalies at each of the red flags, but nowhere else. The money vanished quicker than the pea in a shell game. John drove away as I dialled Sergeant Dave Williams's number. Dave answered quickly. He seemed slightly frazzled.

"Where have you been? I have been trying to get you for an hour. Lionel (Jeffries) is demanding an audience with the three of you soonest." I explained about the school run and volunteered that we could be available for Lionel by two o'clock. Dave asked us to be at the Abertillery police station before two o'clock.

We were shown to the station boss's office. Ian Forbes was the local ranking officer and this was his office. We were invited to help ourselves to tea and coffee. Before we could return to our seats, the door opened and Lionel came in. He looked like the cat who got the cream.

"Derek, Megan, Gwyneth, welcome, please come and sit down." He explained the Home Secretary had phoned him and congratulated him on the Meredith case. After a good chat about the help of the psychic team, Lionel had asked for and received special funding to allow him to purchase special assistance. We were unsure as to why we were being told about this funding. Lionel made it clear. He wanted to purchase our services, thereby ensuring he was entitled to our initial reports. I was annoyed at first, as we had always reported our findings to the police. Lionel put us at ease that we would receive the wages equivalent to the probationary officers and would be given an office with three desks. We would also have access to the police computers and radio channels. The clincher for me was expenses which would include accommodation up to a certain figure. This would pay my hotel bill! The only concession we sought, was free access to the rewards being offered. This was agreed upon. Lionel showed us to an office on the first floor. It had already been fitted out with three desks, a large conference table with six chairs and the walls had three whiteboards with covers. On the table, were three police warrant cards with our details and pictures on them, a badge to be worn externally when needed and three police personal radios. A small instruction card informed us of police radio procedure, and on the back, was a short list of numbered codes for quicker response, such as "officer in trouble" code 10. We moved in before the ladies left for the day. We decided to reveal our latest find in the morning.

The next day Ian Forbes, came in with a young lady named Amy Ford. She turned out to be a solicitor employed by the police to keep them honest. She had three slim files, each with the name of me and the ladies on the front. She presented each of us with our file and asked us to read and sign the Official Secrets Act. We then filled in a form allowing the police to carry out Disclosure and Barring Service (DBS) checks on us. The third form was a contract as probationary policemen, showing our salary and requiring our bank details. The unusual detail of the contract was we were to be paid in advance and termination was by one week's notice for each party. Amy was obviously very efficient, and in fifteen minutes, we were policemen and had been paid. The ladies left for lunch and I drove back to my hotel. The receptionist was a young man, very personable, but a little unsure if he was allowed to reduce my room rate to meet my expenses. The manager, Janet, was more worldly-wise and understood the problem immediately. We agreed on a room rate and a limit that the police would cover as expenses above, which I was to pay on a weekly basis. I asked them to remove the extra furniture to give me back the space and reduce my outgoings, as I was paying for the rental. We also agreed to me keeping the room on an open-ended basis. I sat in the bar and tried out my expenses with a pint.

By two o'clock, we called Dave Williams and asked if he could come and see us. As luck would have it, he was taking his lunch in the Conservative club. Fifteen minutes later, he walked in admiring the size of the office.

"Twenty years and I've got a shoebox, two minutes and you've got a palace." We sat at the table and I asked if he had seen Harry Blackmore's File. He agreed he had but he wasn't sure the facts were correct, as no bodies had ever been recovered. He thought the file was having a go at good hard-working police officers.

I asked, "what if bodies other than Claire Meredith's were to come to light?" His eyes raised to mine and he asked,

"Are there more?" We explained our thoughts and the detectorists' findings. Dave was once again reluctant to call in the cavalry but commandeered two policemen with shovels and we set off to Abertillery Park. We followed Dave's car right up to the start of the path and briefed the two real police on the red flags and their disposition. We were asked to remain in the car as the three policemen went forward. After fifteen minutes, Dave came back and confirmed the first target on the lower path was a small body. He phoned the station and got hold of Ian Forbes, and after a brief conversation, he hung up. He walked back to us just as one of the policemen arrived from the tip and said target two was confirmed as small human skeletal remains. Target three was a dog and target four on the higher path was small human skeletal remains. Three more bodies. Perhaps the black pyramid would now fade from our collective dreams.

The first of the cavalry arrived, a Transit van with a uniformed sergeant and four policemen who closed the site. The sergeant took statements from us, added our newly-given police ident numbers and got our signatures. The remains would have to be carefully exhumed and removed to the morgue. Dave instructed his two policemen to return to the station once they had given their statements and signatures. He gave them his car and got a lift with us. It's a strange feeling finding those little bodies; we should be elated but it was tempered by knowing they were dead and had not met a pleasant end. The ladies went straight home, having already had to organise their kids collection from school. I made for the Conservative Club. Dave had to start a report and raise a file for the finds but I had hardly touched my beer before he walked in. He got a pint and sat down, but before he could speak, his phone rang. It was Lionel. Where were we? Dave explained we were in the Conservative Club. He agreed to join us and Dave asked what his poison was. I had only just set the drink on the table when he walked in, with a civilian jacket over his uniform shirt and trousers. He exchanged pleasantries and got straight down to business. 'Did we know who the bodies in the tip were?'

I replied, 'not yet but I believed they would prove to be from several years ago with several years between each one.' He asked how many would there prove to be. I replied that the best intelligence would indicate a total of twenty-eight to thirty over the past twenty years.

Defensively, he said, "and we have failed to find any of them." Lionel asked how could we have missed it. In answer, I suggested that he should look at communications between counties or even stations. He asked whether I could brief his top teams on Monday morning at headquarters in Cowbridge? I said I could.

"Please make it ten o'clock," a rather dejected Chief of Police said, as he left with little more than a nod to Dave. Dave returned with refills, and as he sat down, he said,

"Please be careful, you have just accepted the poisoned chalice." When pressed, he said the briefing was certainly going to criticise the police at a very senior level. "That would lose you some of the support you may need later in the case." I accepted his warning. We finished our drinks whilst organising the time for golf in the morning. I had a lot of work to do before Monday and had already used up several hours on Saturday with golf.

Susan was already sitting in the bar when I got back. She came up to my room and sat on the balcony as I shaved, showered and dressed. She had booked a table at a select restaurant in Gilwern and decided she was going to drive. I am not a great passenger, believing that I should be the one that controls my destiny. She drove well and we were soon tucking into three courses of superb-tasting food. The food was accompanied by the manager's selection of wines. With Susan driving, the manager allowed me to order by the glass which was a nice touch and kept me slightly more sober. The conversation was light and mainly about the food. Susan dropped me at the hotel about midnight and refused my invitation, reminding me to set my alarm.

The golf was a relief from the rigours of the last seven days. Dave had the advantage of his home course and I ended up losing the best part of a fiver but Dave bought the drink, as is tradition. We enjoyed each other's company, sharing a similar sense of humour and having a similar work ethic. We left the golf course in our separate cars and Dave dropped in at my hotel and I evened up the drinks. When Dave left, I went to my room and started to prepare for the briefing on Monday morning. I made a pot of coffee and began to plan my PowerPoint presentation. Much of the information I was using was directly copied from Harry Blackmore's file. I would need to ensure I had researched the information before presenting it as fact. I finished the presentation, transferring it to a memory stick and ensuring I saved a copy on my laptop. I changed into swimming shorts and grabbed the hotel's dressing gown and slippers. Half-an-hour in the pool and a good shower and it was Saturday night. Susan answered at the second ring, 'did she want to go out?' She said she enjoyed a small music club that showcased local artists. 'Did they do food?' 'No, but the chippy close to the venue was the best around.' I arranged to collect her at eight and called the taxi company. We watched several local acts, both professional and one amateur. All were good and were learning the craft of milking the audience. When we left, I was not hungry and watched as Susan ate fish and chips.

She asked to be dropped at home and said she would pick me up at eight-thirty tomorrow for a surprise day out.

Susan turned up in a riding jacket, jodhpurs and boots. I was dressed in jeans and an anorak.

This looks like horses, and the last time I was on a horse was 1966 when we used to ride the pit ponies, bareback during their two-week holiday (miners' fortnight). It was. With trepidation, I climbed out of the car at Martha's Farm on the banks of Langorse Lake. I was kitted out with helmet and waterproof coat. The mount I was given was the horse equivalent of a Harvey Davidson motorbike. It was squat—my feet almost touched the ground—and it was extremely difficult to turn from its decided path. For all my forebodings, I really enjoyed the morning; the three hours passed in a flash. When we got back to the stables, we tended to the horses, handed back my borrowed equipment and settled the bill. We drove down to Ebbw Vale and enjoyed a great lunch in the newly-opened restaurant, The Lambs Tale. Susan had booked previously but I think we would have been all right anyway if the fuss the maître d' made over her was anything to go by. The jodhpurs gave her, what in riding terms could be referred to as, a good seat. With Susan driving, I took the opportunity to try one of their recommended Portuguese reds. It was the perfect complement for the lamb shank, vanilla ice cream and coffee. I rested my eyes for most of the journey back to the hotel. Susan had things to do so I went down to the pool and floated about for forty minutes. Lying on my bed, I sent Susan a text thanking her for a great day out. I opened up my laptop and checked my PowerPoint presentation. It seemed to be in order. One section of the presentation was a list of young girls missing from South Wales in the last twenty years and matching the timeline that we were working to. I would reproduce the list as a flyer.

Having been with Susan most of the weekend, it seemed strange to be alone for the evening. My Sunday lunch was superb but had been surprisingly light, apart from the wine. I walked down to the hotel bar and ordered a beer. As I sat by the window, I reflected that, not that long ago, you could not get a beer in Wales on a Sunday. I got a taxi and went to the Oaks at the bottom of Oak Street. I chose the Oaks for its location as it was close to the Railway Tavern and the Bush Hotel, and from there, it was only about five hundred-metres to the centre of town. A pint slid down and I recognised no one so I decided to try the Railway Tavern on Bridge Street. The Railway was just across the road from Glan Ebbw Terrace where I grew up. Again, the ordered pint slowly disappeared without me recognising anyone or with no more than a cursory nod from any of the punters. I walked up to the Bush Hotel, and again, ordered a pint of bitter and took a look around. I was the only one that looked like I was drinking. The others seemed to be hotel guests killing time until they could retire for an early night. I had several choices from the Bush but decided to return to my hotel and check the briefing for tomorrow. The taxi dropped me at the front door of the hotel, and as I settled the fare, my phone rang.

Dave asked if I was out. I replied that I was about to be in. I walked into the bar and Dave waved from my favourite table overlooking the lake. Dave introduced me to his wife, Elaine, a tall lady with long blonde hair and a pretty face. She dressed tidily in trousers and a V-necked jumper. Her trainers somehow fitted perfectly with the pint of Guinness she was consuming at a good rate. We chatted for a couple of hours consuming several drinks. Elaine, like Dave, was easy to talk to and the three of us got along famously. By the time they left, I was late for my early night and I would not be checking my brief for the morning. I did manage to get my list of victims printed as a one-page flyer for distribution to the attendees.

# The Angels
## Direct Lift from Harry Blackmore's List.

| NAME | DATE MISSING | FOUND | BURIAL SITE |
|---|---|---|---|
| Claire Meredith | Aug. 2010 | YES | ABERTILLERY PARK |
| Linda Lewis | Dec. 2009 | NO | |
| Christine Olivetti | Feb. 2009 | NO | |
| Imogen Tyler | Dec. 2008 | NO | |
| Margaret Groves | May 2007 | NO | |
| June Thomas | Aug. 2006 | NO | |
| Leslie James | Dec .2005 | NO | |
| Angela Moores | May 2005 | NO | |
| Linda Lloyd | Sept. 2004 | NO | |
| Margaret Hines | Dec. 2003 | NO | |
| Rose Cassidy | Aug. 2002 | NO | |
| Carol Williams | Dec. 2001 | NO | |
| Barbara Amber | May 2000 | NO | |
| Ruby Noble | Jan. 2000 | NO | |
| Pamela Amphlett | May 1999 | NO | |
| Sheila Aubrey | Aug. 1998 | NO | |
| Sandra Morgan | Dec. 1997 | NO | |
| Denise Williams | May 1997 | NO | |
| Lynne Green | Aug. 1996 | NO | |
| Edith Jones | Jan. 1996 | NO | |

| | | | |
|---|---|---|---|
| Laura Smith | May 1995 | NO | |
| Alison English | Aug. 1994 | NO | |
| Jemima Armstrong | Dec. 1993 | NO | |
| Sarah Butcher | Jan. 1993 | NO | |
| Anne Brightwell | May 1992 | NO | |
| Chloe Featherstone | Aug. 1991 | NO | |
| Paris Winters | Dec. 1990 | NO | |
| Leonie Ford | Dec. 1990 | NO | |
| Judy Manchester | Aug. 1989 | NO | |

## Chapter 4

I was a little fuzzy as I consumed my breakfast. I had ordered a taxi for eight-thirty and left myself plenty of time for several coffees. I settled into the taxi and opened the laptop to the briefing. The read-through took only ten minutes which was good. I would extrapolate some parts and have to explain others. With a question and answer it should stretch to forty-five minutes. We arrived at Cowbridge just before nine-thirty. I paid the driver and made a deal for him to collect me at eleven-thirty. I booked in with the desk officer and he directed me to the canteen. There was tea and coffee and the canteen had been set up for the briefing. Tables were set on either side of a centre aisle with the lectern slightly raised at the end of the aisle. Most of the uniforms in the room had silver braiding on their hats. The police in civilian clothes were mostly senior detectives, one or two from each division in the South Wales Police. I was a little nervous as I set up my laptop and ensured it was talking to the projector. As the time ticked towards ten o'clock, Lionel walked into the room and everyone stood. He quickly told them to sit and introduced me. He explained who I was and why he had asked me to produce this brief. He gave me the floor and I stumbled slightly over my first sentence.

Ian Forbes broke the silence with, "don't worry, you are among friends, for now." This elicited a laugh and I relaxed. I explained my background and why I had been asked to assist. I then asked a general question, 'how many young girls have gone missing in South Wales in the last twenty years?' Several guesses came forward, three? Seven? Eight?. I raised my hand and said slowly, 'T-W-E-N-T-Y-N-I-N-E.' The silence was most revealing. I distributed the list of missing angels.

"Some of you will remember these cases, some of you will have been involved in some of them. We have recently discovered the bodies of four girls including Claire Meredith. If my team and I are correct, the killer has operated for twenty years with approximately thirty victims. How has he managed to stay hidden from the police? I believe that, by spreading his victims by location and time, he has convinced the police that these were individual missing persons' cases. As missing persons' cases, the police gave it a short period of intense activity which was quickly scaled back as no evidence was found. Each case was investigated in isolation and the timescales involved ensured that, when and if another child went missing in a specific area, any police previously involved had moved on, retired or been promoted. So, no history was available. Computers were in their infancy and the older policeman always relied on their notebooks. The checking of notebooks was done for accuracy and not for history of offences. If no trending was done between officers in each station, then the chance of anyone picking up trends throughout the Welsh area was very remote. The only person who took an overview was considered a whisky-soaked old hack and Harry Blackmore was ignored.

"I and my team believe we are looking for one man who snatches a victim every eight months, normally during the last few days of the school holidays. We think he films his abuse of the victim and then sells the victim to the highest bidder by secret auction. The winning bidder is then filmed abusing the victim, after which, the victim is killed in a snuff movie. The abductor then disposes of the body. He probably makes £30,000 to £40,000 from the auction and the videos of each victim. He seems to favour certain dump sites, with four bodies in the one site we have found to-date, we can expect a further four, five or six sites.

"You know this person. Certainly, some of you, as younger bobbies, have come across this person; as a peeping tom or animal abuser or stealing underwear or any of the other precursors to murder. You or some of your senior officers could hold the key to the finding of this killer. Now is the time to start co-operating with every division in the Valleys. It may be time to form a task force to collate all the information from all the police divisions. Now is the time for you to use all your experience and collective information. My team will assist in finding the bodies but good policework will be needed to find the killer." The silence as I stepped from the lectern was tangible and I worried that I had failed to convince the audience of the presence of a serial killer in their midst.

Lionel stepped to the microphone and said, "I hope your silence is because you are embarrassed by our collective failure to identify a monster in our midst. Derek and his small team have found four bodies in three weeks. We have found zero bodies in twenty years. Are there any questions for our guest?" An inspector identified by Lionel as Vernon Humfries from Cardiff stood and asked,

" How do you know that all these missing girls can be attributed to one killer?" I considered the question and then answered that it would be very unusual to find four bodies buried in the same location, wrapped in the same type of bed-clothes and closed in a similar black bag and zip fastener. I also believed that, when identified, these young girls will prove to have been killed over a time of approximately twenty years.

Jeffrey Donaldson identified himself as from Port Talbot Criminal Investigation Department. "Derek, this person must have several vehicles. Have you any idea of type or colour?"

"Jeff, not make or colour but I believe he does have several, possibly a four-by-four to access remote burial sites. A snatch vehicle, which could be a "shop" vehicle such as a vegetable shop or fish delivery or an ice cream van. Any van or lorry that is usually seen on our streets and is attractive to children. He may also have access to a motorcycle if he has considered the day when he has been tracked down. The bike could be used for escape along mountain tracks. I will also hazard a guess that some of these vehicles will not be taxed or insured as that would leave a paper trail."

Dave Williams gave me an easy one, "Would you be around until the perpetrator is caught?"

"Thanks, Dave. Yes, my little team of three have been recruited as special advisors and paid as probationary officers. We will be on the case until he is caught or Lionel runs out of money." This elicited several comments, mainly rude, and Lionel stepped in and closed the briefing with a request for the inspectors to give consideration to what they had heard and whether they would like to recommend any of their officers to a task force, if one was to be formed.

I walked out and Dave was at my elbow. "Fancy a pint," I said as I had a taxi coming shortly.

"Cancel it. You will get more feedback in the next hour than in the last month." I phoned the company and cancelled the taxi. Dave gave me a lift to the police local, The Castle Pub in Cowbridge. The landlord opened up with a smile on his face. A couple of hours with thirty or so policemen would be a good start to the day's takings. I noticed Lionel was given his drinks without payment. We mingled with the crowd, stopping to speak to Dave's mates. The general consensus was that it was a good briefing with a shock as to the predicted number of victims. Several top brass expressed difficulty believing that so many police had not been able to link the missing girls. Janice Bowman seemed more interested in psychics than in the proposed task force. She did ask about the timescale and when the next snatch was due and from where. In answer, I replied the next snatch would be in approximately six months and that if we could find the rest of the bodies we may be able to extrapolate where the next snatch would occur.

Just after midday, the police started to fade away. Dave explained that Lionel wanted a task force and they should find volunteers by COP (close of play) today. Dave dropped me at the hotel and refused a drink, saying he wanted to get back so he could put himself forward for the task force. I rang the ladies, who were both doing individual seeing and would be in the office by nine tomorrow. I asked Megan if she had heard from her mother. She was evasive and would only say she had gone away for a few days and needed her privacy. I hung up. I was angry and worried, was this the end of our friendship? I had several hours to kill so rung the gym to see if Arwell was available for a private session. He was running a class at the moment but was free at five-thirty for an hour. I booked him. I went to my room after checking for messages and made a pot of coffee. By seven-thirty, I was in my shower having been beasted for an hour and then swimming for forty minutes. My laundry had been returned and the hanging items were back in my wardrobe and the rest was in a bag on my bed. I sat at the window in my dressing gown sipping coffee. Why would Susan need time away, we had only just met each other after such a long time? We both seemed to enjoy each other's company. Should I ring? I decided to respect her privacy. I dressed and went down to the bar. I fancied fish and chips but they were closed on Mondays. I ordered a pint and grabbed a dinner menu. I ordered a burger with fries. The burger was wonderful—large and juicy—and the salad was crisp and tasty. The fries were thin and well-cooked. I ate slowly and washed it down with a Webbs bitter. There were a few people in the bar but no one looked like they needed conversation. As the clock slowly ticked through nine o'clock, the physical and mental strains of the day started to take their toll. I retired to my room and poured a large glass of my favourite vodka and coke (slim-line) with ice. Sitting by the window, I started to review the day and then the past three weeks. I slept dreamlessly, woke at one o'clock and climbed into bed.

# Chapter 5

THURSDAY morning we met in the office just after nine. Megan took one look at me and answered my unspoken question,

"She will be back home tonight." My phone rang and Lionel asked me to pop into Ian's office. Having already poured the coffee, I took it with me. Lionel, Ian, and Dave sat around a low coffee table. Lionel stood to greet me.

"Morning, Derek. I have decided to put a task force together. Ian will have operational control, but Dave will run the unit day-to-day." My smile must have shown my pleasure at the selections. "Ian will approve any selections put forward by Dave. We will keep the unit small and call on local expertise when it's required. Dave will be expected to provide a report on Friday mornings so, please, keep him bang up-to-date." We left Lionel and Ian to their work and Dave and I walked back to talk with the ladies. Both Gwyneth and Megan were happy that Dave would be our working boss.

Dave asked how we would want to continue after the findings at the Roseheyworth tip. I asked if the bodies had been identified yet. Dave acknowledged that they had not. I proposed that we concentrated on Linda Lewis, aged nine, and chronologically the one who went missing immediately before Claire. Linda went missing during the summer holidays of the previous year and no sign of her was ever found, with the exception of her camera. She was an avid photographer and had several photos published in magazines. From her file, she was a good student. Top groups in all subjects and good at sports, including tennis, netball and cross-country. She lived with her parents, Michael and Joanne, in a three-bedroomed terraced house on Church Street on the outskirts of Newport. It was a Thursday evening and her mother, Jo, had gone off to her job as a barmaid in the Kings Head Hotel a couple of streets from their home. Mike had got interested in a television programme and allowed Linda to play out later than normal. When the programme finished, Mike went to call Linda in. He could not find her. Her camera would later be found on a piece of waste ground. The last few frames showed night sky pictures of the emerging stars. A tyre impression was found close to the camera but an overnight rain shower rendered the print indistinguishable. The loss of Linda put a great strain on Mike and Jo and they had recently completed their divorce. Megan and Gwyneth went off to do the school run—where had the day gone! I took the file back to my hotel room and made arrangements to swim in the sports hall. I got back to the hotel, booked a table for dinner and went up to my room. I put the coffee on and took the file over to the patio doors. Starting from the beginning, I slowly read the file cover-to-cover twice. Dinner was a lonely affair as, deciding to eat early, I was the only person in the dining room. The hotel had a good reputation for steaks so I ordered the fillet with all the trimmings. The waiter, a fifty-something gentleman, asked if I wanted to see the wine list. In response, I asked him to recommend a good red. He returned a few moments later with a Portuguese red. I must have shown a negative reaction. He quickly pulled the cork and said, 'if you don't like it, don't pay.' What could I say to a free bottle of wine? The steak was superb and the red complimented it perfectly. I made a mental note to go with the waiter's choice in future. I also made a photographic record of the label. The wine was Bacalhoa Tinto da Anfora, a rich lively red. I took the remaining wine plus another bottle up to my room. Sitting in front of the patio doors looking out over the reservoir reflecting in the pale moonlight, I reread the file. The wine allowed my mind to drift to a wide street on the outskirts of Newport. Church Street was lined with terraced houses with three and four bedrooms. Between each block of eight houses, an alleyway led through to the rear lane. The street light lit up the area immediately below the lamppost but each lamppost was too far from its neighbour to join up the pools of light. The small shopping complex provided extra lights for the street and this is where the majority of children gathered to play. Between Linda's home and the shops was a small chapel, surrounded by an area that had become waste ground. From the single door, a yellow light showed the hall was in use. I made a note to check if the chapel was in use the night Linda disappeared. A second note was made to check on CCTV in the shops. I opened the second bottle of wine. The local radio station was playing a selection of oldies and I opened the patio doors as the Drifters started into Saturday Night at the Movies. My thoughts drifted back to Newport, watching people walking along Church Street. A van, blue or white or pink? Looking for CCTV cameras. Buses, did they have cameras? Escape routes, back lanes? There was a fair amount of traffic using Church Street but it was slightly later than when Linda was taken. I closed the patio doors as Bob Marley started Jamming.

The wine was a little heavy and I woke just in time to shower and have breakfast before taxiing to the office. The ladies were already seated around the table with steaming coffees in hand. The small talk continued as I got myself a drink. I sat next to Gwyneth across from Megan. Megan was the first to speak. Had I read the Lewis file? I replied that I had and had seen the area of Church Street, noting the amount of traffic, the chapel and the shops. Gwyneth reported similar sights without the chapel and Megan saw the girl lifted as if from a camera close to the shops. We noted our thoughts on the whiteboard and we all agreed to visit the Church Street area that afternoon.

I went back to the hotel and picked up my car. At a quarter-past-one p.m., I picked up the ladies, and following the sat-nav, set off for Newport. Just over forty minutes later, we were parked on the wasteland close to the small chapel. We confirmed our sightings; the houses were in sixes or eights depending on whether they were three or four-bedroomed. The alleys were wide and joined to lanes at the back of the houses. The lanes were wide enough to allow bin wagons or fire engines to access the backyards of the terraces.

We all had points we wished to investigate, so we split up and agree to meet up in an hour. I walked slowly to the shopping centre which was a series of individual shops at right angles to the length of the street. I walked down the pavement on the far side of the road and observed the shopping area. Many of the shops had CCTV but most of them covered the front doors or the small car park at the rear. The front shop adjacent to the road, a barber's shop, had a camera that appeared to cover the length of Church Street. The proprietor of the barber's shop had my defence antenna bristling as soon as I walked in. He was tall and well-built with a shaven head. He was covered in tattoos from the tips of his fingers to the top of his head. I admit I do form opinions quickly, and in the case of Mark Andrews, completely inaccurately. He was a lively character with a great sense of humour and was very welcoming, even when I admitted I didn't need a haircut. His first response was, 'well, something for the weekend then?' I laughed, which was obviously the right response. When I asked about Linda Lewis, I thought I had made a mistake; his demeanour changed and he gritted his teeth.

"If I ever find the bastard that harmed her, I will kill him with my bare hands." I asked how he knew her. He said she always came around, especially when he was quiet. She loved taking pictures. He pointed to the pictures on the wall. Several were of him cutting customers' hair with his tattoos prominently displayed. She could speak intelligently on a wide variety of subjects. She also swept up in the shop and he paid her enough to purchase film for her portrait camera. He said he often paid over the odds so she would be able to get film and take her pictures. I asked about his CCTV and he said he had already given the police a copy. When I explained about the different police departments, he understood completely and offered to rip off another copy. He asked me to come back in thirty minutes. I walked back to number ninety-six and had a brief look in the alley and back lane and then made my way to the chapel. There were no sounds emanating from the chapel but I tried the door, and to my surprise, it opened with a loud screech. A rather young-looking cleaner asked if she could help me. Her name was Marion and she cleaned the chapel two evenings a week. She said the choir did not meet on a Thursday night and the chapel was normally locked and only she and the chapel custodian had keys. She did clean on a Thursday but tried to get it done between four and five-thirty, so she would have locked up and gone before Linda was snatched. After cleaning, she put tea for her family and got ready for her open mike night. She was a singer and was trying to get noticed in the local scene. I thanked her and walked slowly back to the barber's shop. As good as his word, he handed over a tape. As I walked out, I thought that if I lived locally I would enjoy his company.

I dropped the ladies at their cars so they could collect their children and agreed to see them tomorrow. I went back to the office and asked for an IT expert. Jane knocked on the office door and introduced herself. She was a special advisor to the police for IT matters. She had worked here for nearly eighteen months and was a graduate of London University where she got a first. When I explained what I needed, she confirmed the time and date of the disappearance. Twenty minutes later, she returned with the tape and a CD. The CD was labelled with the police number and case ident. The tape was also labelled in the same manner and had an evidence custody number, and from now on, needed to be signed into evidence, and if it was required in the future, would have to be signed for. I took the tape downstairs to the desk sergeant and signed it in. Jane showed me how to load the disc and how she had partitioned it to start running one minute before the scenes of interest. I ran the disc from the start but soon got bored, and making the required keystrokes, teed up the scenes of interest. The camera was pointed north along Church Street, the streetlights were not brilliant and images were often fuzzy and out-of-focus. The images I needed were often out-of-shot or blocked by vehicles travelling along the road and the camera was also flashed by vehicle headlights. The road had a slight s-shape as it approached the camera which, for short periods of time, would mean that larger vehicles would completely block the camera's view. The images moved slowly and then showed a young girl playing on the pavement, sometimes hopping, as if in a hopscotch square, and sometimes holding her hands up, as if framing a shot for her camera. In one place, the lights of a vehicle appear in the alley next to number ninety-six. The vehicle stops and the lights immediately go out. Between vehicles on Church Street, the internal light on the target vehicle illuminates briefly. A person is seen coming from the vehicle, grabbing the young girl and returning to the target vehicle. The internal light illuminates briefly and goes out. The headlights come on and the vehicle reverses up the alley, turns into the lane and drives off. The camera is thrown out at the wasteland. We don't know why. Maybe dropped in the alley and moved by someone else later. There was no CCTV camera cover of the alley or the waste area.

The next morning Dave came to see us. He needed a report of our work with any progress and any planned direction of investigation. We told him how we hoped to concentrate on Linda Lewis. Her aura would be the strongest as she was the one taken immediately before Claire. We showed him the CD and asked if we were being given access to all evidence in these cases. He assured us we were. I then made him aware that the police had been given a copy but it was not available on-file. Dave watched the video several times and made a note to find the original copy. Dave also confirmed that the other three bodies had still not been officially identified. I joined the ladies at the large table made of our three desks. We discussed our way ahead and decided to try the Inert Earth Crystal Pendant. Gwyneth spread the large-scale map over the desks and pinned it securely around the edges. I carefully unpacked the pendant and tripod. We chose our current position as the starting point. With the pendant hanging vertically, we sat close and joined hands, close to the desks. After five or six minutes of concentration with Linda Lewis as the target, the pendant started to move. The infinitesimal movement slowly increased until the momentum moved the tiny wheels on the tripod. Each movement of the tripod slowed the pendant's swing and then the process started again. I knew that the pendant would continue to operate until it centred on the energy we were seeking. It could take some time. We left the pendant crawling towards an unknown target and took our lunch break. I drove back to the hotel and parked close to the door. I wasn't hungry and decided to walk around the reservoir. The day was pleasantly warm with a gentle breeze coming off the water towards the hotel. The path around the lake is approximately a mile-and-a-half so I stepped out briskly and completed the circuit in just over twenty-five minutes. I went up to my room and sorted my laundry. I was back in the office in a little over an hour. The pendant was still moving so I turned on the computer and looked for e-mails. Susan had mailed me late-morning and wanted to meet for dinner and drink this evening. I replied in the affirmative and asked where and when. I didn't want to seem over-enthusiastic but I was very happy that she was back. The second mail was from Dave. Could I pop in and see him? I logged off and walked down the corridor to his office, he was out. I walked back along the corridor as the ladies came in. We made coffee and sat around the desks watching the pendant. Megan asked if Susan had contacted me. I said she had but only by e-mail and only to ask me to dinner. Megan seemed reluctant to continue with the conversation. We talked through what we had seen in Church Street and we were convinced we had seen the actual abduction, but regardless of how many times we watched the video, there was little in the way of evidence to be gained from it. Little did we know that the investigation was about to increase in pace and intensity. We left the pendant to run overnight and I went to the pool for an hour. My mobile rang as I got back to my room, it was Susan.

"Could we meet in The Oaks at seven o'clock? Megan and John will join us because I need their support." The terminology scared me and I realised that I was not looking forward to this meeting. I showered and dressed in clean jeans, a white buttoned-down shirt and a grey jacket with a blue check. I went down to the bar just after six and ordered a beer. I sat at my favourite table overlooking the lake, and no sooner had I taken a mouthful, than Dave turned up. I joked he must have smelled the beer and heard my wallet open. I got his drink on my expenses. He indicated that I was smartly dressed and I told him I was meeting Susan and it may be the end of our relationship. I ordered a taxi and Dave told me the reason he had come to see me. The bodies had been identified and the cause of death established. The report would be passed out in the morning. The Oaks Hotel took its name from the street on which it stood. It used to stand opposite the railway station before the Beeching Review. The lounge of the Oaks was fitted out with booths around the wall overlooking the street. Each booth had its own small window out onto the world. I understood why she chose this establishment if she wanted to talk about personal issues. As I entered the lounge, Susan met me half-way across the floor, she flung her arms around my neck and kissed me smack on the lips. She led me to the booth and slid in, leaving me to sit on the outside. John came back from the bar with a pint and I thanked him and swallowed a good mouthful. The silence was slightly awkward so I started,

"Can you now tell me where you've been?" Susan took a drink and told me she had been to Addenbrooke's Hospital to see a specialist cancer surgeon. I felt sick. She said she was diagnosed with a malignant breast tumour. The doctor at Addenbrooke's had examined her and assessed her suitability for a procedure he had developed, whereby the cancerous material was removed and the reconstruction, including the insertion of the implant, was carried out in one operation. If all went well, she could be home within a day or two. Everything was going well until the nurse started filling in the paperwork and then the price was mentioned. Even with a very generous loan from John and Megan, Susan was unable and unwilling to pay that much. It would take most of her savings and she had little or no chance to replace any of that money for future expenditure. She had come home with a reservation for Monday afternoon and she needed to confirm or cancel by noon tomorrow. I refreshed the drinks and we ordered our meals. Once we had settled down, I took Susan's hand and asked if she would let me pay for the operation and any other expenses. The quiet tears running down her cheeks informed me that I could. I think John and Megan would have given up the money gladly but were happier realising they did not have to. After dinner, John and Megan took their leave with John shaking my hand and Megan hugging me. Later, on the deck, leaning against me, Susan asked,

"How will I get to hospital? Will I have to go up on Sunday or will Monday be early enough?"

I replied, "Leave it to me and I will get you there on time."

The golf was good and Dave and I took money off our opponents but it was evened up, as usual, by the purchase of drinks in the bar. The weather took a wet turn as we left, and arriving at the hotel, it was throwing it down. I leapt out of the car and took the steps two at a time. Dave was right behind me.

"Well, you are on expenses," he volunteered. I ordered the drinks, checked my car was locked and joined Dave at a table. We had hardly sat down when Ian Forbes came in. I asked what he was drinking and fetched it from the bar. Ian asked if I'd read the post-mortem reports. I said I preferred to wait until the ladies and I could read them together. Ian gave me a precis of the reports and included the names and snatch dates of the subjects. He asked if I could explain why there was such a long time between burials. I thought for a minute and said,

"Do you remember my last briefing?" He indicated that he did. I said,

"This probably means one of two things. He either brings the victims back to a burial site close to their homes and feels safe with the site as it has never been discovered. Or he has several sites already picked out before he starts killing and he dumps them in his sites according to their snatch date. We should be able to say which it is by looking at the list of the missing." He took a minute to work his head around this and then said,

"Well, we will look at this on Tuesday then. I understand you have arranged for a day off on Monday." I said that was right and Dave was going to check terms and conditions to see if we were entitled to holiday. He replied that if we weren't, he would personally authorise it and to, please, give Susan his best wishes. He stood and I thanked him and he shook my hand before leaving. I sat back down and looked at Dave. Dave said,

"He is interested in your team and in you particularly. He is always asking how you work and what instruments you employ. He likes the idea of psychics and has asked if you could help on any other types of cases. You have a fan, Derek, and a powerful ally, if you ever need one." My thoughts were somewhere else when Dave put two pints on the table and sat down with 'one for the road.' Dave asked after Susan and I brought him right up-to-date.

When Dave left, I showered and sat on the deck outside my room; the rain had left a fresh clean smell in the air and the coffee aroma was sharp. My thoughts went to Susan and whether she feared the upcoming operation. The alarm let me know it was time to get ready. Casual dress was difficult for me. In the Air Force it was polish, shirt and tie and creases in trousers. Mucky, I can do. I have been described as a dirt magnet, so torn jeans and twenty-year-old t-shirts are normally de rigueur. I settled for a short-sleeved shirt in blue with black chinos and dark brown loafers. I grabbed a three-quarter raincoat and met Susan in the car park. She drove silently to the club and parked and then, taking my arm, walked me across the road to a small bar. She asked for a coke and smiled at my quizzical look. I ordered a pint, and as it was being poured, she said no alcohol until after the op. We found a table, and when seated, she started to ask me about the travel on Monday. I told her about Dusty and his charter business. We would be sharing the outbound flight with a jockey who was going to Newmarket to ride out on the gallops. I would arrange to fly back when she was settled in or when the op was complete. I would need to collect her at seven-forty-five Monday morning. She smiled but I knew she was apprehensive. We walked to the club. It was a long time since I had been stamped with a black light fluorescent stamp. We were early and there were several tables empty. Susan chose one toward the back of the room, close to the bar but away from speakers. I could imagine this room years ago; it would be brown with cigarette smoke. A great law change meant it was now much easier to smell the pot. The evening was very pleasant, with several good acts and some enthusiastic amateurs. I love a sing and my throat was sore when we left. Susan supported me back to the car and poured me out at the hotel. She decided not to stay; can't say I blame her. It was Sunday tomorrow so may as well have one more.

We were invited to John and Megan's for Sunday lunch. I left the hotel early and called in at the supermarket ,where I picked up flowers and chocolates for Megan. I was sitting in my car looking over the Vivian Street area, when Susan opened the car door. She kissed me gently and laughed, "good mouthwash, I need to stop for flowers," and laughed again when I pointed out the things on the back seat. John and Megan lived in a large three-bed semi on Richmond Road. They had been lucky as the previous occupants had converted the rear of the property to a large kitchen, diner with a large island and bi-fold doors to the garden. Lunch was lamb, Welsh, with mint sauce and three vegetables, topped off with gravy, like mum used to make. The meal was offered with a choice of cold drinks; Susan chose coke and I decided to stick to beer. John, Megan and the two children had orange and lemonade. I was full after the first course but Megan had worked so hard that I could not refuse the Eton mess. I did not refuse the cheese and biscuits and picked at them until it was time to leave. John and Megan were good hosts and very easy to talk with. They asked about the trip to Cambridge and I explained the logistics of getting Susan to and from Cambridge. Megan's eldest, Sonia, asked if she could go in the aeroplane. I made a note to see if the return flight to collect Susan was exclusively ours. It was soon the polite time to leave and we thanked our hosts and the children and I drove Susan to her house. She invited me in for coffee and we chatted for some time. She was worried about the operation and would prefer to have company for the evening. We packed her case for the hospital and added items for the evening. Sunday was an awkward night for finding food but we had eaten our fill, and if we could not wait till breakfast, the hotel would be the best place to get bar food. At the hotel, we stole a few newspapers, ordered breakfast for six-thirty and went to my room. Susan made coffee and we sat inside next to the windows. By eight o'clock we were restless and went down to the bar. We played pool for an hour but Susan was uneasy. We were just about to call it a night when Terry and Sheila came in. The company was very convivial and we were soon in good spirits. Sheila and Susan were niece and aunt, but as there were only two or three years between them, they were more like cousins. They talked about everything and nothing whilst Terry and I played pool. Terry was still working at the family building business so needed to be in bed fairly early. Whilst I had the opportunity, I asked him to keep an eye out for a good four-bed house. He said he would. We waved them off about eleven and went up to my room. I stood looking out of the patio doors and considered how lucky I was to have secured this room with a fantastic view of the lake. Susan came out of the bathroom all wrapped up in hotel towels and I knew I was lucky. I slept dreamlessly which was unusual for me. The alarm clock was followed quickly by the automated alarm call from the front desk. We jostled and danced for the toilet and shower, and by six-thirty, were entering the breakfast room. The young lady named Judy took our order; a full English for me and toast and cereals for Susan. The pot of tea was placed in the middle of the table. After breakfast, we cleaned our teeth and placed Susan's case in the car. A final pit stop and we left slightly early but we didn't want to rush; I think Susan was still slightly apprehensive about flying.

# Chapter 6

RHOOSE International is a small ex-military airfield that was a satellite unit for St Athan. We turned into the airfield and were cleared by the airfield security and drove to the Brothers Charter hangar on the east side of the airfield. Dusty was outside prepping the Piper Aztec. We parked and Dusty came over and gave me a hug. In military terms, he hadn't changed one bit. In actual terms, his hair had become a lot greyer and his waist had thickened more than some. He asked if we had any luggage and we showed him. He took the case, weighed it and loaded it into the plane. We went inside to a waiting room and he provided us with tea. Susan asked how long the flight would be and he answered, 'about sixty-five minutes if the wind remains constant.' There was one other passenger in the room and I introduced myself to Shaun McMace. He said he was glad to share the cost. He was a young jockey who was doing a lot of training for established trainers for very little money. This, hopefully, would be his last year as a rider and then he would qualify as a jockey. I asked if he had bagged the front seat or if I could have it. He said he hated flying and needed to be in the back. I introduced him to Susan. The Aztec had been taxied to the front of the hangar and was parked with the number two engine running. A young girl completed our next-of-kin forms, and as soon as she was happy, she walked us out to the aircraft. I got in first and took the right-hand front seat. The captain always sits in the left-hand seat. I put the headset on and Dusty confirmed the doors were shut and started the number one (left-hand) engine. He called the tower and got permission to taxi for runway two four. We would be taking off towards the southwest. Dusty asked if we were all happy and strapped in. He asked whether I had flown a twin. I had not. He said, 'I'll do radio, you taxi on and take off!' The radio crackled and line up and hold was permitted. I moved the throttles forward and steered the aircraft onto the centre-line of runway twenty-four. Checked the magnetic for a heading of two hundred-and-forty degrees. Throttles to idle, toe brakes on, flying control checks. Radio, ready for take-off. Tower, clear for take-off. Throttles coming up, engine instruments check, in the greens, brakes off, centre-line, engine greens, throttles open. The aircraft leapt down the runway.

"Seventy, eighty, ninety," Dusty read out our speed. As we touched ninety, I eased the stick back slightly and the nose wheel left the runway, at ninety-five knots, the aircraft lifted gently into the air. Straight ahead to three hundred feet, check rate of climb, raise flaps in stages and select gear up. The aircraft gathered speed and altitude. As we passed one thousand feet, I reduced the throttles to ninety percent and Dusty radioed our call sign and change of heading, turning left onto 090, climbing to five thousand feet. I eased the control stick to the left, and keeping a good eye on our altitude, turned the aircraft slowly to an easterly heading; 090. I checked the trim and set a climb for five thousand feet. Dusty called in a change of radio frequency for our onward flight and then confirmed a basic service with our transit radar service. Dusty took control, to the relief of the other two passengers. Susan came on the intercom and said,' I didn't know you could fly.' I said, 'I have a pilot's licence but it has lapsed.' She bashed me and said, 'you scared me.' I said that Dusty was following every move I made. Dusty chirped in and said the only fault would be two hundred feet undercarriage up. I replied I had never flown a moveable undercarriage. We flew gently in good weather over the river Severn and followed the M4 east to Swindon, turned left to 040 degrees for Oxford, then onward south of Milton Keynes and to the south of the huge hangars at Bedford. Changing frequency to Sibson Airfield, we used instruments to locate beacons close to Cambridge, and finally, landed at Sibson. Taxiing to the light aviation hangar, Susan and I got out and retrieved our case. Dusty popped in to sort out the landing fees. We agreed I would phone before sixteen hundred hours(four o'clock) to cancel or when I leave the hospital to get a lift back today. It was eleven o'clock as we got a taxi to Addenbrookes.

Susan was booked into the hospital. Her case was taken and her clothes were shaken and hung in a wardrobe, the smalls were put tidily in drawers. The doctor turned up in minutes. He examined Susan and spent the next fifteen minutes explaining the next four days. The operation would be today. Tuesday, rest and dressing change. Wednesday, examinations and exercise. Thursday, exercise, inspection and home plan. Leave hospital Thursday afternoon. Susan turned to me and said, 'you need to go back to work.' I held her close and said, 'any problems, please, call me. I can be here in three hours.' She promised she would and ushered me out of the door. I rang Dusty from the taxi and he said he would be back at Sibson in forty minutes. The Aztec curved gracefully over the M11 and descended to the runway. It taxied onto the dispersal in front of the light aviation hangar. Dusty shut both engines down and climbed out. We pushed the aircraft to the fuel pumps and zeroed the delivery gauge. Dusty put fifty litres in each wing tank and disappeared into the office to sign the visitors' book and pay for fuel plus landing fees. He phoned in the change of time on his flight plan. We pushed the aircraft away from the pumps and climbed aboard. 'Still happy to handle the take-off,' Dusty asked. 'Yes,' I said. Dusty got permission and started the engines. Dusty asked for permission to taxi to Point Alpha for power checks. We taxied to the hold point, turned into wind and applied the brakes and increased engine power to one thousand revs per minute, checked the mag drops and dropped the revs per minute back to idle and checked the flying controls. Dusty radioed ready for departure. The reply, hold short at alpha. We watched as a small feeder airliner landed. The tower then called with our call sign and we were cleared for take-off. We lined up and increased revs per minute to maximum, rocketed down the runway and lifted off. Gear up, flaps up, climbing to five thousand feet on two hundred-and-forty degrees. The M4 crossed our path and we turned slightly to follow it. As we crossed into Wales, Dusty took control and reduced power and altitude as we approached Cardiff. We carried out a standard overhead join and were soon taxiing to a stop right outside the hangar. I went into the office and completed the paperwork including the payment. I quickly thanked Dusty and mentioned I may need to go up on Thursday and bring Susan home. I was back at the hotel by five and called Gwyneth. She said she and Megan had reset the crystal from a point to the south of the indicated point, and by the time they left, it had travelled back to the same point as previously. I said, 'see you tomorrow,' and hung up. I rang Megan and talked about her mum. She was concerned but I told her she was in good hands and she would be home Thursday. I rang Dave and he said he was just going to the Conservative club. I rang my favourite taxi company, and fifteen minutes later, was sharing a pint with Dave. We talked about post-mortems, which I was still to read, and about Susan and the operation. Dave then asked if I had any update on the case. I told him that we may have identified a second burial site but we could not confirm it until we had walked the ground, possibly tomorrow. He asked if he could come along and maybe bring my new fan, Ian Forbes. I said I had no objections and that a second Land Rover would make sense. We could organise it in the morning as I wanted to review the work of the ladies before we leave. Dave replenished my glass and left. I would need to be on top form so a swim and an evening meal saw me sitting in my room by eight o'clock. I telephoned Susan and was surprised at how cheerful she seemed. Megan had already rung and they had spoken for a good while. She understood we may have discovered a new burial area. I said we would need to be walking the area with Gwyneth and her rods in the morning. The operation had been a complete success and she was already walking around in a very padded training brassiere. We exchanged pleasantries and she excused herself for being tired. I mixed my favourite vodka and coke and sat looking out over the reservoir. I climbed into bed just before ten o'clock.

Ian Forbes climbed out of his car just as I parked. We walked up to the top floor together, and as we got coffee, he asked if we were going for a walk this morning. I said, 'if the ladies' work from yesterday is sound then we will be walking the ground. I have yet to read the post-mortems and then we will decide. I'll give you a call about nine-thirty.' I read and reread the post-mortems. Apart from names, addresses and dates, they could have been photocopies. Violent sexual abuse was suspected, but as the bodies were skeletal, the only real evidence was the scoring of the front face of the third and fourth vertebrae inflicted by a heavy blade with a serrated edge. The ladies came in at nine-fifteen dressed for a mountain walk. They hung up their coats and collected drinks. Megan asked about Susan and we talked for a few minutes. I then asked about the second run of the crystal and Gwyneth stepped up to the map. She indicated a point well south of where it now stood. She had circled the start point and noted the start time, nine-thirty, within the circle. It had taken some time using only the energy of the two of them to initiate the crystal. By ten-fifteen, it was obvious the crystal was moving the tripod. They left it in a locked office over the lunch hour, and when they returned, it was still moving. They reread the post-mortems while the crystal continued to move. At three o'clock the crystal had stopped, and when they checked the position, found it to be at the same spot as the first run. I was satisfied the ladies had been precise in their handling of the second run. I phoned Ian and said we would be walking a certain area and would be happy for him to accompany us. His disappointment could be heard in his voice.

"Sorry, Derek, I have a pressing problem but Dave has made himself available. Please keep us all informed." We made our preparations for departure, borrowing shovels and made sure we had proper footwear, a flask of coffee and a few chocolate bars. Dave was tied up for an hour and decided to let us go on our own. He would follow if we found anything—glory grabber. The ladies arranged for the kids to be collected at three-fifteen and sorted for the school to give them lunch. Gwyneth and I climbed into the Land Rover. Megan decided two vehicles would be better than one. We would make further arrangements in the nearest town to our target area. We stopped in Treharris.

The ladies took advantage of the facilities and I purchased three bottles of water. We asked about the condition of the roads up to Clydach reservoir, and being told they were all good, we decided to continue with both vehicles. The road topped the mountain and flattened out, passing over a cattle grid onto a wide plateau dotted with squares of fir trees. Each square was about two hundred metres long. The regimented impression was at odds with the meandering ribbon of the road and the irregular outline of the reservoir. At a point where we had the first square to our left and the reservoir to our right, Gwyneth asked me to stop. She got out of the Land Rover and walked slowly towards the trees, turning to her right, she walked parallel to the square of trees for over one hundred metres and then stopped. As I drove up to her she said, 'not this one.' We continued along the road and stopped again at the second square of trees. Explaining this was the vision she had seen, she exited the Land Rover, divining rods in hand. Megan and I pulled our cars off the road and got out. Gwyneth walked the road edge of the square with her rods held softly in front of her. She reached the end of the square of trees, and shaking her head, she turned and walked slowly back towards us. She said,

"There is something here," as she passed us and walked towards the southwest corner of the plot. She had got within thirty metres of the corner, when the rods swung hard right, and following them, Gwyneth disappeared into the square. A path, almost hidden from the road, ran for forty metres and then opened into an oblong space about ten by twenty metres. Gwyneth looked back at us with a strange look on her face that said, 'I have found something, but I am scared.' Both Megan and I closed up for support and Megan readied the red flag markers. Gwyneth walked the oblong twice and then started her third lap. This time, Gwyneth stopped and Megan took her cue and marked the position. This was repeated six more times. Looking back at the clearing, the red flags were evenly spaced along one side of the clearing. Gwyneth was emotionally drained but I asked her to do one more lap. She understood that she would not have to concentrate on the areas of finds this time but could just survey the more general area. She found nothing more. We collected the shovels and the water, and moving to the area of the first marker, started to dig. We found the black plastic sack at a depth of only forty-five centimetres. Manipulating the bag, it was obvious that the contents were human, small but human. As soon as we were positive about the contents, we contacted Dave Williams. Dave returned my call to say he would hand this to the local crew, and a few minutes after I hung up, we heard the sirens coming up the mountain. A plain car and Ford Transit drew up alongside us and a plainclothes officer got out. Sergeant Mostyn Evans introduced himself and his two policemen and asked me to show him what we had found. As we walked down the access path, he said Dave trusted me but he didn't know me so he would have to play it by-the-book. He hoped I would not be offended. I said, 'no offence would be taken,', and as soon as we were confident we weren't wasting the police's time, we would leave the site. He nodded his agreement with our actions. We reached the oblong and I explained that each marker was a possible grave and we had dug part of the first site to ascertain that it did, in fact, contain human remains. Mostyn asked the policemen to secure the site and asked us to return to the vehicles. The Transit returned from the far end of the plot where they had placed POLICE NO ENTRY SIGNS. Mostyn opened the rear doors and retrieved a briefcase. He took out three witness forms and had us complete a statement, which were signed and dated. As we were paid policemen, our numbers were added. Mostyn then opened the site log, made several entries which brought the operation up to date. He was just telling us that we could go now if we needed to be elsewhere. Before we could move, Lionel's car powered over the hill. Mostyn was taken aback as Lionel spoke to the ladies and then shook my hand with a, "well done, Derek, how many?" I answered, 'seven.' He spoke with Mostyn and made sure the procedures were being followed. He beamed when he found everything in order.

"Mostyn, Derek, walk with me." When he had seen the site, he shook everyone's hand and started for his car. He stopped and called me over. "Derek, you must be concerned as to what is happening with the police task force in support of your case. I have been asked to give a big drug case priority, but I am very pleased with your progress and Dave will be back with you tomorrow." He got into his car and left, just as the recovery and forensic teams arrived. In quick time, they cleared the site forensically. The recovery teams retrieved the seven bodies with all burial materials, including the earth, in very short time. It was just as well, as the clouds were rolling in and the rain was already falling,

We decided it was time to leave, so we checked out with the site officer. Mostyn waved as we drove off. The ladies had both gone in Megan's car, which left me with an empty car. I picked up the shovels and drove slowly back to Abertillery. The drive gave me time to ring Susan who answered immediately. She was in a good mood; the recovery was going very well and the pain was controlled. They already had her in a soft training bra and were continuing with physio. It still looked like home on Thursday. I told her about our success in the mountains and she agreed to fly home if possible. When she hung up, I rang Dusty and expressed my interest in flying to and from Sibson on Thursday. Dusty took the booking, saying he would sort something out. Dave rang as I drove into Aberbeeg and onto the new road; new to me. He asked if we could meet before he finished for the day. I said I was free and only had to return a couple of shovels, which could be any time today or tomorrow. He suggested the Conservative club in fifteen minutes. He had already got the beers and a table out of earshot of anyone else. I asked him what was going on. He said,

"Two drug gangs in Cardiff had made it clear that people should keep clear of a certain area on a certain date and time. The police had decided that it would be a feather in their cap to take the gangs down. The armed response units were in position and the gangs turned up with a large cache of drugs. A young policeman gave away the element of surprise. In the ensuing gunfight, four gang members were killed and one officer wounded. The fall-out is causing ripples right up the chain. We may not be able to give you the support your good work deserves." I completely understood. I asked if we were able to call out the cavalry ourselves if we made any progress. He said Ian Forbes had asked if we could put our investigation on hold until Monday. I agreed if we could carry on doing work in the office. Dave agreed. He finished his drink quickly and left. I drove to my hotel. The gym had an hour free with Arwell and he gave me a good workout with the emphasis on stretching. The pool was almost empty so forty minutes of swimming breaststroke left me in a relaxed mood. I showered and sat with a coffee, wondering what tomorrow would bring.

Wednesday. I delayed getting into the office until a quarter-past-nine. The ladies came in just after me, and once the coffees were sorted, I bought them up-to-date with the information Dave had given to me. I asked them to review the work we had done, putting names to the bodies from Roseheyworth tip, seeing if the bodies were dumped close to home or in some sort of rotation with other burial sites. And if it was by rotation, did it give us a calculation of how many sites are being used? Once we had answers to these questions, we should concentrate on the next missing body chronologically, Christine Olivetti.

If any of us needed a day off this would be a good time and we would have no problem getting it authorised. Megan, being the one with the neatest handwriting, chose to annotate the boards. Gwyneth and I took the post-mortems and hunted for the facts that Megan chose as important.

By two o'clock in the afternoon, we had what I considered was concise information for the first four recovered sets of remains;

| Claire Meredith | Aged 7 | Abertillery | Missing 30 Aug. 2012 | Found 24 Sept 2012 | Abertillery Park |
|---|---|---|---|---|---|
| Angela Moores | Aged 8 | Tradegar | Missing 13 May 2005 | Found 24 Sept. 2012 | Abertillery Park |
| Ruby Noble | Aged 8 | Llanilleth | Missing 7 Jan. 2000 | Found 24 Sept. 2012 | Abertillery Park |
| Sarah Butcher | Aged 7 | Pontypool | Missing 14 Jan. 1993 | Found 24 Sept. 2012 | Abertillery Park |

From this small list, we saw that the bodies were deposited each six to seven years apart and we could expect five sites to be used. Apart from Claire, they were not close to their homes so we could realistically say the sites were pre-selected and bodies deposited, in turn, at each site.

We pulled the file on Christine Olivetti. She went missing in February 2009. Her case was given the similar pattern of searches; family, neighbours and friends, police for approximately seven days, with searches then wound down and no evidence ever found. Christine lived in Tynenewyedd, a small town in the Rhondda valley. During February, the evenings were short and the nights dark. Children were normally indoors before dark. It would, therefore, be interesting to know why she was out so late. She was at the top end of the preferred age range, being nine when she went missing. The police report ruled out the distraught parents who were fourth-generation Italian. The great-granddad was an Italian prisoner-of-war who never went home. The family were into ice cream vans and Italian restaurants. This family had put up the largest of the rewards, £50,000. So, it would be nice to find their daughter. The girl had gone missing three years ago so would we get anything more from further interviews? Perhaps we should just play the inert earth crystal pendant card and see what comes through. From the file, it seemed that Christine was always running errands for her infirm granddad, and that evening, she had gone to the shop for his rolling tobacco. The shop knew the family circumstances and sold the tobacco to the girl knowing it was not for her. On the return walk, she had gone missing. The pouch of tobacco had been found, either discarded by the girl as a clue or thrown out by the killer as he had no reason to keep it. There appeared to be no CCTV and only the minimum number of interviews, with family, friends and neighbours. The reward was offered by the granddad and guaranteed by the Western Mail. The police appeared to give up after a week; they seemed to form no hypothesis or persons of interest. The case went cold long before the weather got warm.

Before we left for the day, we set the inert crystal over Tynewyedd, the small town in the Rhondda, and waited until it showed signs of motion. We locked the office and asked the desk sergeant not to let anyone in overnight. The ladies left to do the school run and I popped into the Conservative Club. I was halfway through a pint when a person sat down at my table! At first, I had trouble placing the face but a repaired cleft lip put his name into my head. Jim Bryant was a force of nature when we were young. He was always bigger than the rest of us and he was a year older than me. He was the first of our gang to own a car, a Fiat 500, the original one. Jim may have been bigger than everyone else but he was a good soul who never bullied anyone. He allowed me to drive his pride and joy from Abertillery Park, down Glandwr Street and Carlisle Street. Jim had joined the army at the time I had joined the Air Force. We sat for an hour and caught out up on each other's lives. Jim had done the whole time in the army and retired with a decent pension. He still swallowed his beer quickly and said he had heard I was in town as the Merediths were family. Looking at his watch, he excused himself and said he was due at the Conservative club's annual general meeting which was tonight and he was the chairman. We promised to keep in touch and I gave him my card. I got to my hotel just before eight o'clock. I phoned Susan; she seemed a bit down. She was not recovering as fast as the surgeon had hoped. The latest estimate was to leave hospital Friday morning. She was worried that it may cause problems with collecting her from Cambridge. I told her not to worry, that I was sure Dusty would sort me out, and if he couldn't, I would drive up Thursday and bring her home as soon as she was discharged. I wanted an early night so I ordered a burger and chips with coleslaw from the bar, washed down with a pint. The coffee was bubbling when I got back to the room. Taking a large mug, I sat by the patio doors that were almost closed against a Welsh shower; it was throwing it down. The wind and rain ruffled the surface of the lake, and if it wasn't so late, I would have called Dusty and rearranged my flight. I washed my mug, stripped and climbed into bed. Sleep came quickly.

## Chapter 7

ON Thursday, I checked with Susan and the prognosis was still the same. The best guess was Friday midday. We chatted for several minutes, and when I hung-up, I dialled the number for Dusty. He was immediately on the defensive,

"Derek, I don't have an aeroplane for today so is it possible to rearrange for tomorrow?" I was tempted to string him along but something told me it was serious. I agreed it could be Friday, to be at Cambridge Sibson for midday. He agreed and I hung up. Breakfast was a full English with white toast and tea. I arrived at the office just after nine, and unlocking the door, I noticed the crystal had changed its position. I marked the position on the map and wrote the co-ordinates onto the whiteboard. The ladies came in and quickly organised coffee. We repositioned the crystal over Christine Olivetti's house and sat holding hands until the crystal started to oscillate. We finished our coffee as the crystal moved very slowly over the map. While we read the files of the missing angels, the crystal drove the tripod slowly towards an unknown target area. After lunch, the crystal was stationary over the same point as the previous run. The area was near Newbridge, to the south of the A472 and to the west of Celynen Street. It looked like access would be difficult, as the area was being logged but the coroner and local police made short shrift of any complaints and all work on the site was shut down on the authority of a local magistrate. After consultation with the police, it was decided that our work on the site would not start until Monday. This would not jeopardise our operation and meant forensic and coroner's offices would not need to work over the weekend. It would also give the forestry commission time to clear the site. We would work on the next burial site through today and take a three-day weekend, returning ready to walk the site on Monday. I cleared our day off with Dave and he reminded me we had a four-ball on Saturday. I would be there.

After lunch, the ladies had chosen to read the file of Pamela Amphlett. Pamela was seven-years-old in 2004. She was playing out the last week in July after breaking up for the summer holidays. The weather was warm and the evenings were long. Pamela's parents were in their neighbour's garden having a barbeque. The neighbours were a young couple who had no children, and so, Pamela was given permission to play with her friends who lived about fifteen houses down the street. At about eight-fifteen, Pamela's mother went to look for her. Not seeing any children in the street, she knocked on the door of the children Pamela had been playing with. The children's mother said she called her girls in at seven-thirty as they had not eaten and she did invite Pamela to eat with them but Pamela had said she should go home. Fifteen houses, one hundred yards, forty-five minutes which cost the girl her life. Nothing was ever found; no CCTV, no witnesses, NO HOPE. Once again, a missing persons case, fruitless searches by family, friends, police and many church groups, St Johns, the scouts and local rugby teams. The searches were scaled down and the files moved from active desk to archive shelf and then to storage. The speed with which the authorities forgot, only added to the family's anguish. The lack of any repeat cases was proof of the police's belief that she must have wandered off. It also served to calm the fears of the populace. The only history of Pamela outside her family was collected by Harry Blackmore at the Western Mail.

Pamela lived in the small town of Oakdale. She had been a precocious little girl who loved performing. She would perform songs and dances at the drop of a hat. She loved entertaining her family and friends and her favourite present had been her karaoke machine. It was her ambition to become a singer in a band.

Once we had identified the bodies in the second and third burial sites, we would use Pamela, if she was still not found, to allow the crystal to detect her burial site. We made our annotations on the whiteboards and closed the office down for the weekend. I phoned Dusty to confirm the aircraft was available and I could bring along an extra passenger. Susan was in a good mood when I rang. The recovery was back on track, and failing anything unforeseen, she would be released after rounds at ten o'clock tomorrow. She had been up and around all day making tea for patients and staff. She was still uncomfortable but felt so much better following a shower and a trip to the hospital's hair salon. We discussed the arrival time for me—Sonia was a surprise for Susan, a happy one I hoped. She asked about my plans for the evening and I had to tell her that I had none. It would probably be gym, pool and hotel meal and an early night. I hung up after promising to check with her before leaving for the airport. Arwell was moving the exercise intensity up a notch or two and several areas of my body ached as I swam gently for forty minutes. I showered and considered crawling into bed. I dressed and went down to the bar. A table near the television was free and there was European football being shown. I had no real interest in either team but as Billy-no-mates it looked like I was interested. My favourite meal of a burger and chips was washed down with a lovely pint of bitter. I was twitching around from the sudden cramp in my left thigh when a couple entered the bar, and after a brief conversation with the barman, approached my table. They politely introduced themselves and asked if I was Derek Rowlands. I confirmed I was and asked them to join me. I got them drinks and asked them what I could do for them. The lady spoke,

"You have already done enough for us. We are Kathleen and Mervyn Noble. Ruby, our daughter, was one of the bodies you discovered at Abertillery Park. She was missing for twelve years and now we can give her a proper send-off." Mervyn spoke for the first time.

"Derek, I am a wealthy man and we have come to offer you a reward for doing what the police never could." I stopped him in mid-flow

"Mervyn, the police were disadvantaged by the location and the lack of organisation in the valleys. Your daughter was one of thirty angels taken by a skilled predator who honed his technique over twenty years, snatching a girl every eight months. Each girl was taken towards the end of the week so the weekend would be inconvenient for police and civilians. It was also the last week or so of the holidays so, once the missing person's case was elevated to murder, most people had forgotten each girl as they prepared their own children to return to school." He looked a little dejected but absorbed my words before getting up to replenish our drinks. Kathy was a lime and lemon, "I'm driving," she volunteered. Mervyn returned with our drinks and said, what about our offer of a reward? I told him of the deal that we had with the police and the rewards already offered by the Western Mail and the insurance companies.

"Please keep your money, and if you want something to remember Ruby by, why not set up a scholarship to a university for one of your villages less fortunate?" Kathleen and Mervyn finished their drinks and promised to set up the Ruby Scholarship. They were ecstatic with the outcome and thanked me again for finding their daughter and for the suggestion of the scholarship. I watched them to their car and kept watching until they drove from the hotel grounds. I could not help but think why such terrible things should happen to such nice people. My next two pints seemed to disappear very quickly. Once again, my early night was not to be.

Morning came quickly and I phoned Dusty to confirm the aircraft was available. He asked that we arrive to be airborne by ten-forty-five to guarantee Cambridge for midday. So I needed to leave by nine-thirty. I rang Megan and asked if Sonia still wanted to go in the aeroplane. From the shrieked reply I assumed she did and arranged to collect her at nine-twenty. I drove to the office and read through the information we had accumulated on the site near Newbridge. I also checked to see if the post-mortems were in for the lake site; they were not. Closing the computer down, I made my way to Megan's and collected Sonia. I stopped at the local sweet shop and purchased some sweets in case she didn't like flying. Dusty was all business and by ten-forty we were airborne. The flight was uneventful and we touched down at five-minutes-to-Twelve. The taxi dropped us at the door of the private wing of Addenbrooke's and we walked through to the reception desk. Susan was in the day room and waved as we stood at the desk. I reminded Sonia not to jump up at her nanny. She was superb. She ran to Susan and stopped and waited for Susan to extend her arms before she hugged her. I kissed Susan lightly as the tears ran down her cheeks. She had been released and we could go straightaway. Susan said her goodbyes around the ward and we arranged a taxi back to Sibson. Dusty was ready to go and we were airborne again just before one o'clock. Susan and Sonia hugged all the way back. They talked incessantly and it was apparent that Susan was flagging as we landed at Rhoose. We completed the paperwork, climbed into the Land Rover and drove slowly back to Six Bells. We dropped Sonia into her mother and Susan excused herself and asked to be taken home. I dropped her at her home and asked her what she wanted to do. She said she needed some time to herself. I said she didn't need to be looking after herself and she should come to the hotel for a few days. She saw the sense, and after repacking her case, we drove to the hotel. Janet was on duty in reception and I let her know that Susan would be staying for a few days and that if she needed to charge for double occupancy to please put the cost on my half of the bill. She said, "I will check but I doubt if we will charge, apart from food." We unpacked her case and she asked for some time to herself. I phoned the gym and got Arwell for an hour and swam for half-an-hour. I knocked on the hotel room door and used my magnetic key when I got no answer. Susan was in my favourite chair right in front of the patio doors. She was fast asleep. I closed the bathroom door and showered and shaved, then dressed in a hotel dressing gown. I poured myself a vodka and coke. I dressed, making sure Susan was covered up, opened the door and sat on the patio overlooking the lake. It was eight o'clock before Susan woke, she walked out onto the patio and sat on my lap. She kissed me and said, "thank you for everything. I am tired but I am hungry as well. Can we get a meal in the bar?" She washed gingerly and we went down to the bar. It had been a long day and a small meal and a few beers were exactly what we needed. Susan was still on anti-biotics but chose to have a couple of drinks. I told her I was playing golf tomorrow morning but we could go and get her car if she needed it. I told her it was an early game and that I would be back in time for lunch. She said she would sleep in and have a shower in private. I asked if she wanted to cancel the room cleaning service. We agreed to delay it, if possible, or cancel it, if not. We put our request to the front desk and they agreed to cancel the room servicing in the morning. We slept together but apart and I was awake long before the alarm clock went off. I showered, put a pot of coffee on and dressed and went down to breakfast. I came back thirty minutes later with tea and toast and Susan was sitting up in bed. She looked a lot better for a night's sleep. I gave her the tea and toast and pointed out the filter coffee. I put my mobile number on her speed dial. I kissed her gently and left for golf.

Dave and I were together against two of his long-term friends. Gordon was a flooring salesman and Martin was a plumber. My antenna twitched as I realised I would need tradesmen like these if Terry ever found a house that met my requirements. I tried my best to ingratiate myself with them but Dave played so well that we took their money. As is the tradition with golf, the winners buy the drinks so Dave and I were out of pocket as we left the course. Dave came back to the hotel and had one for the road on my account. Somewhere in the conversation, he mentioned that Lionel, the Chief Superintendent, had mentioned a briefing for Tuesday morning and had implied I was to be the guest speaker. This was news to me but not a complete surprise. It was the reason I kept the PowerPoint files and report up to date. Dave left just before two o'clock. I popped up to my room and found Susan sitting, looking out over the lake. She looked tired but smiled in a contented fashion. I made coffee and we sat looking out at the view for some time. I asked if she fancied dinner out somewhere. She answered, 'yes,' but this afternoon she would like to visit her parents' graves. It was the anniversary of her father's death. He had died in the explosion at Six Bells Colliery in 1960. Her mother remarried and died some twelve years ago. Both had been buried in Brynithel cemetery. We popped into the local florist, got some flowers and then drove up to the cemetery. I remained a little way away as she paid her respects and laid the flowers. Susan then called me over and proceeded to introduce me to her parents. I wasn't sure whether I was supposed to ask their permission to be with their daughter. She seemed less tired as we left the cemetery and she asked if we could visit a place that was special to her. How could I refuse? She directed me along small roads and then an unsurfaced track. The trees, mainly Scots pine, parted as we crested a rise onto a small flat area no bigger than a rugby pitch. The view was spectacular, with hills on both sides of a valley covered in pines, rolling down to a small village nestled in the valley. The small river running through the village looked silver in the late afternoon sunshine. The church looked much too big for the size of the hamlet. We walked arm-in-arm to the edge of the clearing and sat quietly for what seemed ages. As the lights in one of the cottages came on, we realised we needed to leave. We drove back to the hotel. I was flagging a bit as we walked to the hotel. Susan asked if I really wanted to go out. I gave it some thought and said I think I would prefer to stay in the hotel. Her smile said, 'I agree.' We sat in the bar with a beer and I told her I thought her dad and mine may have known each other. I told her my father was an engine driver and was normally on the same shift as her father. There were two engine drivers on each shift and they operated the static engines that pulled the tubs or coal drams from the coal face to the lift shaft so that they could be lifted to the surface. The day before the explosion, my father was asked to swap shifts with his opposite number so he could attend a family event in the afternoon. My father agreed and was at home the morning that the explosion occurred. It seemed as if our lives were meant to be entwined. We ordered bar food and a second beer. We played pool and drank beer until eleven and retired to our room like an old married couple.

Monday morning and we gathered in the office. Coffee in hand, we held a quick review of the Newbridge information. The site was cleared and secured and the site office held the keys. A quick phone call confirmed the site office was manned and they were expecting us. We travelled in two cars. Megan and I in the Land Rover and Dave and Gwyneth in his official car. Dave spoke to the security office and we were granted access. Gwyneth stood in the gate area and surveyed the site. Her head was tilted as if she was trying to trace a tiny noise. The site was on a slight hillside. The high area was to our left with the land sloping to the right and dropping away as it receded into the distance. A small river bordered the right-hand boundary immediately before a main road. Gwyneth stepped through the gates and crossed the concrete car/equipment park. She paused briefly and pulled the divining rods from her pocket. Standing stock still, she allowed the rods to swing freely in her hands. Slowly, the rods settled in a general direction to the left of the site. Following the rods, Gwyneth walked slowly uphill to an area that seemed to be devoid of tree stumps. Gwyneth walked away from the entrance gate for several hundred metres. At a point where the ground took a more pronounced slope, the rods swung through one hundred-and-eighty degrees, back the way she had come from. Gwyneth placed a green marker at the point and walked back towards the gates even more slowly. Megan had joined her and was now placing red markers at each point where Gwyneth stopped. Gwyneth visibly relaxed and we all realised she had completed her task. Looking along the hillside, the markers seemed to be equally spaced but slightly further apart than those in the reservoir site. Dave chose the closest marker and started to dig. Within minutes, he had uncovered a black plastic bag and ascertained that the contents were small and human. Dave walked back to the security office and told them what had been found. He used the landline to request the forensic and recovery teams. We had found a further eight angels but needed to have them identified before we could proceed with our enquiries. The ladies and I drove back in the Land Rover, leaving Dave to brief the recovery teams. We made out our reports and signed them in the presence of the desk sergeant. The ladies left sharpish to pick up the children.

## Chapter 8

WE were now waiting for the results of the post-mortem examinations of fifteen bodies. The seven from the reservoir site and the eight bodies recovered from the Newbridge site. The results would, we hoped, identify each individual body thereby giving us the date of abduction, family witnesses and the area where they spent their short lives. It would also give us a steer as to which angel we should concentrate on for the remaining burial sites. Gwyneth and Megan had spent several hours reading up on Pamela Amphlett but she would be identified as one of those found in the lake site. The results we needed would not be available for ten days, give or take. Susan was getting more comfortable by the day, and with ten days to fill, I suggested we take a trip to Norfolk. I needed to start to prepare for my move to South Wales . My attic and garage were so full of stuff that I would need to take several trips to the tip with a small lorry. My wife's clothes and possessions would need to be sorted and sent to charities or kept for my daughter and granddaughters. The house that Terry had sourced for me was coming along and I would soon need to put my house on the market and enter into a firm commitment to buy the house in Cwmtillery.

Susan picked me up at seven o'clock and we drove to a small pub in Cwm. This was my choice, as my great-grandfather had lived in Railway Cottages, Cwm, when they moved from Somerset to find work at the turn of the century. As the tin mining petered out in the southwest of England, the coal mining was starting to provide employment in the Welsh Valleys. We walked the small area of Railway Terrace and I took several photos of the small cottages which I knew housed at least nine people in their early days in Wales. The pub, The Railway Tavern, seemed to come from a much more modern time. Light wood, glass and contrasting dark floor tiles made a welcoming sight. The landlord and landlady were equally welcoming, and in no time, we were settled at a corner table away from the jukebox and pool table and furnished with our choice of drinks and the evening menu. The fare was mainly steaks, burgers and several vegetarian dishes. The thing that always amazed me was the catch of the day. Wales was never known for fish but it seemed that, wherever we went, the fresh fish was fantastic both for taste and value. I settled for red snapper and Susan chose a veggie burger. The beer was lively and maintained a good head right down the glass. Susan chose a small glass of white wine recommended by the landlady. It was crisp and fruity and proved a wonderful companion to the vegetarian dish. We skipped dessert and ordered coffee. We had both eaten dinner at a rate that suggested we needed to talk. I went first, reiterating my wish to return to Norfolk to move my house sale along and invited Susan to accompany me for the week. Her reluctance told me she had an alternative and it was more to her liking. Megan and John had rented a cottage down on the Gower peninsular and had invited Susan for a rest and for extra childcare. I understood and agreed she should go and enjoy her grandchildren. We agreed that the week would allow me to get on with the house and give her at least some rest. Susan dropped me at the hotel and I watched her car lights disappear with a heavy heart. I went to the bar for a pint of solace. I also arranged with the hotel to hold the room vacant for a week. I rang Megan and Gwyneth to say I would arrange for police leave for the next week and we could resume on the following Monday morning. I then spent an hour packing my kit into the car. The next morning, I spoke with Dave and cancelled the golf for the next two weekends and received permission to take the week off. By ten-thirty a.m., I was on the road back to Norfolk. The next week was a blur. My housekeeper proved to be a godsend. With my permission, she had sorted my wife's clothes and all I had to do was take them to a charity shop. The garage and attic were more of a job but the internet soon gave me a contact for house clearance. After two phone calls, I agreed with a local firm to clear my house of anything that remained when I left for Wales the next week. A storage company would arrive Monday with large storage crates to pack anything I wanted to move to my new home. Sunday, I managed to get to my local golf course and play with my old friends as a member of the HOGS (Honourable Old Golfers

Society)—there are other less polite descriptions. Sunday afternoon, I dismantled electrical equipment around the house, drained petrol mowers and emptied sheds. My tools were packed in large boxes while I left the workbench for clearance. Back to the internet for the fish—I have a fish pond in the garden with goldfish. It's hard to find people who are willing to take fish other than Koi. A Graham Young rang on Monday and said he would take the fish. An hour later, he came around to look at them and said he would take them when he could if he could also have the pump and filter set up. It was a no-brainer. My gardener, who was also my neighbour, agreed to obtain soil and hardcore and fill in the pond once the fish had gone. We agreed on a price and I paid him against the future work.

Monday morning I was up early. The storage company had given me adhesive labels to put on each piece of furniture to be stored. I thought I had sorted everything before they turned up but I had to make several decisions as we went around each room. My bedroom threw up a problem. I needed my king-size bed to go but did not want to sleep on the floor. The village had several bed and breakfast establishments but they were not within walking distance of pubs and restaurants. I chose the Bridge Hotel in Coltishall village. There are four pubs in the village and three of them are recommended eating houses. By Thursday morning, my house was cleared and my fish had gone. I felt lonely so phoned Susan. It was great to hear her voice and Megan and John shouting from the background. They were going home on Saturday and I agreed to get there Saturday. The estate agent arrived at ten o'clock and quickly walked through the house. He asked if I needed a quick sale and I answered, "not really." He gave me his valuation, and after a brief discussion, we settled on £475,000, hoping to realise £460,000. I gave him a set of keys and the contact details of the housekeeper who had the second set. I went to the Recruiting Sergeant for lunch and confirmed with Mathew that I could have a table for thirteen for dinner that evening. I invited my friends from the village and we had a good night. Mathew was a great host and the food was epic. The front-of-house service provided by Nichola and her daughter was faultless and their generosity with the wine at cost was fantastic. My friends drifted away about ten o'clock and I found a quiet table in one of their garden pods to savour a pint of bitter. My credit card almost bent double as the wireless machine sucked the money from it. Ten minutes later, I was in bed and fast asleep. Friday morning, I walked down to the river and sat watching the ducks. I was slightly hung-over and in need of a drink. I returned to the hotel and ate a decent breakfast. After several coffees I felt almost human. I drove back to my house and let myself in. It was eerie; the house felt so empty and quiet. I contacted my housekeeper and ensured she could continue to keep the place aired and clean until sold. We agreed on a schedule and price and I transferred an amount that covered some arrears and a few weeks of future work. She also agreed to hold any spare keys and I collected all the keys and took them to her. The house was no longer mine.

I paid my hotel bill and arranged that I could leave early Saturday. Dinner was in the Kings Head and I walked next door to the Rising Sun where I sat at a table overlooking the River Bure. Susan was packing to return home tomorrow. She sounded relaxed and admitted she had enjoyed being with the family and was happy that she had been useful in looking after the grandchildren, teaching them about rock pools and the animals that could be found therein. We agreed to meet for dinner at my hotel. I rang the hotel and confirmed it was available. I ordered another pint and drank it slowly. A pleasant evening stroll back to the hotel and a large coffee while I packed my kit into an already crowded car. I was asleep just after ten. Dropping the keys into the hotel box provided, I left Coltishall at half-past-four. I was always surprised by the amount of traffic on the roads even in the early hours of the morning. For the next five hours, I drove steadily westward towards Wales. The Severn Crossing is the beginning of the end of my journey. Forty-five minutes later, I parked in the hotel car park as close as possible to the deck adjacent to my room. The car took an hour to unload and reminded me to sort out some storage. Finally, at eleven-fifteen, I sat in the hotel's bar and ordered tea and toast. My phone rang as I poured my second cup of tea. It was Dave Williams, the usual banter tempered with a hint of concern; had I sold the house, how did I feel, etcetera. Then the real reason for his call—the post-mortems on the Newbridge site victims were complete and copies had been locked in my office. From a police perspective, they were of very little evidential value, almost photocopies of the previous reports. From my point of view, they would indicate how he chose his burial sites and in which order he selected his search areas. It would also allow us to focus on the latest victim not already accounted for. I told Dave I would pop into the office and read the post-mortems and then drop into the Conservative club about one-thirty. His reply, as expected, was, "I'll see you there." I called the taxi firm, and ten minutes later, I signed into the police station. The office seemed lifeless and dark, so I switched on every light and the tubes lit up in order down the length of the office. The whiteboards stood out starkly and the names of the victims identified from the first two burial sites shone accusingly at me. I retrieved the post-mortem files from the locked cabinet and sat at the large table. I got myself a glass of water and opened the first file. The next hour was a sickening time of reading a complete repetition of reports I had read from the previous burial sites. With the exception of dislocation of wrists, elbows and shoulders from suspension injuries, the post-mortems could have been from any of the previous burial sites. The suspension injuries were a departure from the normal modus operandi. Dave was waiting in the Conservative club when I walked in. He shouted me a pint, and I took a long swallow before I sat down. Same MO?" I agreed. "How many recovered now?" I replied, "nineteen. The worst thing, is none of them were pleasant endings. Death may have come as a relief." Dave nodded as we emptied our glasses.

"What is your next move?" I answered slowly,

"We will wait until Monday and speak with the ladies. Then we will consider how he operates and try to figure out who of those still missing we can best track back through time and space to give us a clue as to their current whereabouts." The second pint was more social and we covered golf, Susan and my house sale, even for a copper he was nosy but he was becoming a very good friend. Then the shocker—a young man had walked into a police station in Port Talbot with a VHS tape that appeared to show one of our angels being abused and killed. The young man and his wife were house-clearing after her father had passed away. The tape cassette covered in red tape had caught their eye and they decided to view it before disposing of it. Their first impulse was to burn it and preserve her father's reputation. However, the pieces in the recent copies of the Western Mail led them to believe this could be important. They were interviewed under caution but were honest and their actions proved their innocence. Dave indicated the tape had been copied twice. Copy one was sent for professional inspection and copy two was now available for viewing at the station by authorised personnel. We finished our drinks and prepared to leave, when Dave said, "are you eating out tonight?" I explained Susan and I were eating in the hotel. Dave then invited us to eat with him and his wife at the Oaks, nothing special, jeans and jumpers. With that, the date was sealed. Dave and Elaine waved as soon as we entered the bar. True to his word, both were dressed in jeans and jumpers. Susan and I had chosen jeans with short-sleeved shirts. The evening flew by; good food and company lubricated with several drinks and last orders came all too early. Susan wanted to spend the night in her own home so Dave and Elaine gave her a lift and I called my favourite taxi company. Sleep was difficult with visions of victims and post-mortem reports, buildings of every description, including a strange tower.

The days were blurring into a fast-moving diary. Susan was recovering more each day. The pain medication had been reduced to the point where she could decide when and how much. With Susan's attitude, this meant no medication unless she screamed. The scars were getting less vivid with each passing day and she was now able to wear her normal bras as opposed to the training items she was supplied with. This was doing wonders for her self-esteem. On Thursday we drove up to Addenbrooke's for her three-week check and the scan and blood test came back clear. We booked into a hotel in Milton Keynes and invited my daughter, Jo, and her partner, Bernie, to dinner. Jo was wonderful and she and Susan were soon chatting like old friends. By ten o'clock, Susan was flagging, and we decided to call it a night. Jo and Bernie hugged her gently and my daughter whispered, "she's lovely," as she kissed me goodnight. Susan and I took our drinks through to the bar and sat quietly for an hour. When Jo rang to say they were home, we finished our drinks and went to our room. Breakfast was excellent and we were on our way just before nine o'clock. We meandered home, keeping to A and B roads, avoiding the Severn Bridges by driving around Chepstow. We made Six Bells at about three o'clock after stopping for a light lunch at a delightful pub on the banks of the river Wye. Dropping Susan at home, I drove to my hotel only to find she had left me a message saying, 'rugby club tonight, will pick you up at seven.' The second message was from Dave Williams arranging golf for Sunday morning.

Unbeknown to me, Susan was a long-time member and supporter of the Abertillery Rugby Club. She was also, until very recently, the club treasurer. Everyone we passed had a nice comment for her. A couple stood and waved as we entered the lounge bar. Susan led the way through the tables and greeted the couple with hugs and kisses. I was introduced to Jim and Dianne. Susan explained that Jim had taken over from her as treasurer and Dianne, with the help of several others including Megan, had been instrumental in the forming of the ladies' team. I went to the bar and got the round in; Susan caught me and said another pint and a Campari and soda. As I deposited the tray on the table, I was introduced to Greig and Anne. Greig was a banker who worked with Susan and Anne was Susan's riding buddy. They were a talkative bunch which suited me as I tend to be on the quiet side. The theme of the night was song and laughter. A male singer kicked things off, followed by a comedian and then a local male voice choir. I refrained from singing but I really enjoyed the evening. At about eleven-thirty, Susan indicated that she needed to go home and we took our leave. I sang in the car.

We both slept soundly and I got up just after seven. I took Susan a cup of coffee and shaved and showered. At breakfast, it was obvious there was something on her mind. The young girl brought our toast and tea to complement our cooked breakfast. Susan spoke before I had a chance to ask what was wrong.

"I really enjoyed last night and was really happy you fitted right in with my friends."

I replied, "it wasn't difficult as I enjoyed their company but it was really due to me being with you that gained me their acceptance." She said she had been away from home for long enough and wanted to go home after breakfast. I said I would take her home. I didn't know how I felt, so posed the question "are you still happy to be with me?" She took my hand and said, "more than happy but I have a house to look after. I also want to invite Megan and John for lunch. You will come, won't you?"

"Yes, please."

Susan directed me to the local supermarket where she stocked up for the year. We then drove down to Lancaster Street. While she unpacked the shopping, I made coffee. My domestic skills stretched to pushing the vacuum around and peeling the potatoes. Susan finally got bored with trying to keep me entertained and preparing the lunch, so she kicked me out. My strict instructions were to be there by one-thirty and "don't be drunk." ME?

I dropped into the Conservative Club for a pint but there was no one I knew. I decided to swim and went back to the hotel. My room seemed empty without Susan and I quickly got changed and went down to the pool. Several swims interspersed with jacuzzi and the time flew by. I showered and dressed; shirt, jeans and new loafers. I popped into the bar, and to my surprise, Terry and Sheila were sitting at the first table. I asked what they were doing. They surprised me by saying Susan had invited them to lunch and they had been instructed to collect me and provide me with a lift to and from Susan's. I remember peeling a lot of potatoes, now I knew why. We nursed a pint for a long time, and finally, we were able to get in the car and set off. Sheila was a good driver and we arrived in good health with hardly a dent in the car. Two of Susan's friends from the rugby club were there and we re-acquainted ourselves with each other. Susan gave me a big hug and laughed at the bewildered expression on my face. She asked me to enjoy the afternoon and all would become clear. The afternoon was lovely. Jim and Dianne, the couple from the rugby club, were very good company. They regaled us with stories of their travels and also of their nights in the rugby club. Sheila remembered more of our escapades back in the sixties. Susan served a fantastic roast beef meal. Her only mistake was asking me to carve, but eventually, all the guests got a full plate. We ate and drank our fill. A Chateau Neuf de Pape was demolished in minutes only to be replaced by another. The dessert was a light and tasty roulade. Coffee was served and my offer of washing-up was rejected. Susan stood at the end of the table and called for silence. She thanked everyone for coming and thanked Megan and John for organising childcare for their two children. She recounted her experiences of the past six weeks. The diagnosis of her cancer, the appointment with the doctor at Addenbrooke's, the meeting with an old boyfriend, the hospital admission and the recovery. The lunch today was to thank everyone for their support over the past six months. She walked around the table and pulled me to my feet. My smile was only cooled by the tears that ran down my cheeks. I kissed her passionately and we slowly began to dance to music that appeared as if from nowhere. The other guests joined us on the dining room dance floor and all moved to the rhythm of the music.

After an early breakfast, I flew to the office. I had access to the post-mortems and spent the first hour reading each file again. The ladies arrived just after nine and began to read the files. By ten, they were up-to-date and I asked Gwyneth to set up the TV and VHS tape player. I went downstairs and got permission to view the tape and signed it out from the evidence locker. I briefed the ladies and ensured they wanted to view the tape. The first viewing was horrendous and all we saw was the sexual abuse and the murder of a very young girl. After subsequent viewings, we were able to look for flooring, wall coverings, the abuser's clothing, build and characteristics, any chance reflections or accidental features identified on camera.

By midday, we had watched all we could take. The ladies left to do the school run. I, in need of a drink, walked to the Conservative club. Dave was one minute ahead of me and sat with Ian Forbes with three glasses in front of them. Dave called me over and presented me with a pint, "knew you would need this.". Ian asked if we had gained anything from the tape. I thought for a minute before answering,

"It's not the first time he has filmed it. There seem to be no reflections or accidental identifications, there are no clocks or windows, there are no sounds other than those forced from the victim. The client is masked but naked, this means a changing room, and possibly, a shower facility. The bedding appears to be the same as the wrappings inside the black plastic bags we have recovered." I settled back and took a drink whilst Ian gave Dave that, 'well, I never,' look. Dave said,

"We are impressed that you picked up all that. It's the sort of report we had hoped for from the psychologist."

I replied, "I had hoped they would provide us with more."

Ian said, "Don't hold your breath." The afternoon went quickly. Megan updated the List of Angels that had been recovered and identified. From the list of the missing as supplied by Harry Blackmore, we had recovered nineteen. This left eleven to find. From the number of bodies in each of the previous three sites, it led us to believe that we were still looking for two more sites.

The ladies were starting to clear their desks for the end of the day, when in walked Harry Blackmore. We had not thought about the rewards since we were enlisted as paid policemen and women. Harry was his normal joyous self.

He quickly listed the girls found that carried a reward and dropped four cheques on the desk. The total was £110,000. We were astonished; even with our deal with Lionel for the Police Welfare Fund, each of us had just received £27,500.

Tomorrow would be an interesting day!

# The Angels

| NAME | DATE MISSING | FOUND | BURIAL SITE |
|---|---|---|---|
| Claire Meredith | Aug. 2010 | YES | ABERTILLERY PARK |
| Linda Lewis | Dec. 2009 | NO | |
| Christine Olivetti | Feb. 2009 | NO | |
| Imogen Tyler | Dec. 2008 | YES | NEWBRIDGE |
| Margaret Groves | May 2007 | NO | |
| June Thomas | Aug. 2006 | YES | CLYDACH RESERVOIR |
| Leslie James | Dec. 2005 | YES | NEWBRIDGE |
| Angela Moores | May 2005 | YES | ABERTILLERY PARK |
| Linda Lloyd | Sept. 2004 | NO | |
| Margaret Hines | Dec. 2003 | NO | |
| Rose Cassidy | Aug. 2002 | YES | CLYDACH RESERVOIR |
| Carol Williams | Dec. 2001 | NO | |
| Barbara Amber | May 2000 | YES | NEWBRIDGE |
| Ruby Noble | Jan. 2000 | YES | ABERTILLERY PARK |
| Pamela Amphlett | May 1999 | YES | CLYDACH RESERVOIR |
| Sheila Audrey | Aug. 1998 | NO | |
| Sandra Morgan | Dec. 1997 | YES | NEWBRIDGE |
| Denise Williams | May 1997 | NO | |

| Lynne Green | Aug. 1996 | YES | CLYDACH RESERVOIR |
| --- | --- | --- | --- |
| Edith Jones | Jan. 1996 | YES | NEWBRIDGE |
| Laura Smith | May 1995 | YES | CLYDACH RESERVOIR |
| Alison English | Aug. 1994 | NO | |
| Jemima Armstrong | Dec. 1993 | YES | CLYDACH RESERVOIR |
| Sarah Butcher | Jan. 1993 | YES | ABERTILLERY PARK |
| Anne Brightwell | May 1992 | NO | |
| Chloe Featherstone | Aug. 1991 | YES | NEWBRIDGE |
| Paris Winters | Dec. 1990 | YES | NEWBRIDGE |
| Leonie Ford | May 1990 | YES | NEWBRIDGE |
| Judy Manchester | Aug. 1989 | YES | CLYDACH RESERVOIR |

# Chapter 9

GWYNETH had updated the data on our main whiteboard and the name of Christine Olivetti was the latest victim still missing. She was also the most rewarding from our point of view. The Italian family made their money from ice cream vans and shops. They were one of the first vans to use the Mr Whippy-style machines to dispense their product. The reward for information leading to the recovery of Christine was £50,000.

Tomorrow, as it turned out, was not very interesting; Lionel called a briefing for his top staff to be brought up to date and invited me to lead it. Dave Williams had been asked to provide the police perspective and he was in our office to pick my brains as soon as I walked in. I gave him a quick run-down of the up to date figures and data that Gwyneth had collated. Dave always wanted to have all the information at his fingertips, but as I was also giving a briefing, I kept my summations to myself. I asked the ladies to read the post-mortem reports and see what they could elicit from them if anything. I also suggested they reread the file on Christine Olivetti and see if they could use the inert earth crystal to indicate her final resting place. By ten o'clock I was happier with my briefing slides, and as I started to assemble my bits and pieces, the bow tie and braces of Harry Blackmore walked in. Could each of us give him a one-hour interview today? It wasn't a question. I explained about the briefing and he asked if he could have the ladies this morning and me after lunch. We agreed; after all, he was the paymaster general.

The briefing was lively but we all stuck to the rules of courtesy. Dave laid out the history of the case and came right up-to-date with the latest finds and our part in it. I then explained the burial sites and how the victims had been circulated between the sites, sometimes by chronology, sometimes by geography, and occasionally, by the killer's belief that a particular site was safe. I featured the video and commented on the lack of evidence we had been able to get from it. The forensic psychologist's report had, to my knowledge, not been received. Ian Forbes confirmed this and agreed to chase the report. I then gave them my feelings and beliefs for the next weeks. I thought there would prove to be another two burial sites based on the numbers we had found in the previous sites. I thought my team and I would locate the sites in the next fortnight and then, in collaboration with some good police work, the killer would be found within a month of the last site being forensically cleared. Lionel stood and thanked both Dave and me and urged his officers to give as many resources as possible to find the killer.

"Dave Williams is head of the task force and now that the other problem has faded, he needs some of your best men."

The briefing lasted until lunchtime and I dropped the briefing slides on my desk as Megan finished her interview with Harry. It was decided that Gwyneth and I would be done after lunch as the ladies left for the school run. Gwyneth shouted over her shoulder, "crystal's running." I invited Harry to the Conservative club for lunch.

We returned at about one-thirty p.m. and the ladies were both at the map table looking intently at the inert earth crystal.

Megan looked up and said, It's stopped!" I walked to the table, and after several minutes, I confirmed the crystal had indeed stopped. I had to submit to the interview with Harry so instructed Megan and Gwyneth to rerun the crystal from a different location after marking the start and finish of the first run. As the ladies positioned the crystal, Harry and I made ourselves comfortable in the big chairs.

Harry already had a lot of our background information so today was to cover the discovery of the burial sites two and three; Clydach Reservoir and the site at Newbridge. Harry allowed me to ramble and only interjected when my version differed from the story that, I was beginning to believe, he had already written. By two-fifteen p.m., I was released and Gwyneth took my place. I walked over to check on the crystal and Megan confirmed it was still moving. For the next thirty minutes, I sat quietly and contemplated the visions of buildings and a tower. It looked like a factory site but old and dark in a sinister kind of way. Nothing was coalescing into clear thoughts so I made coffee for myself and Harry as the ladies prepared to leave for the day. Megan asked if I'd seen her mum recently as, when she saw her last, she seemed down. I admitted I had not seen her for a couple of days but was picking her up for dinner tonight. I promised to be aware that she may not be in the best of moods.

I carried the coffee across to Harry who had not moved an inch since lunchtime. I asked, politely, if our interviews were giving him enough to get on with. He replied he was very happy and his editor was pleased with the content and increased circulation. When Harry left, I checked the crystal was still moving, locked the office and asked the desk sergeant not to let the cleaner in. With an early finish, I rang the gym to see if there were any trainers available, only to be told no. So I did an unsupervised session of forty minutes and then swam for twenty minutes. Returning to the hotel, I made a coffee and sat on the deck. The thoughts of buildings and a tower persisted but no progress. I phoned Susan, who sounded well up for a night out. Abertillery is not a huge place so finding locations to eat and drink was getting somewhat problematic. After giving it some thought, Susan rang back to say we were off to Pontypool to a small bar/restaurant then to a comedy club. She was driving.

The next morning, the ladies arrived minutes after I had unlocked the office. The inert earth crystal had completed its second run and we all studied its final resting place. The pendant was perfectly centred above the pencil circle that Megan had used to indicate the termination of the first run. The small village at the centre of the circle was typical of many in the South Wales coalfields. The cluster of small houses was originally built to house the management of the mine which dominated the immediate area. The mine was one of the deepest in the Welsh coalfield and its existence was the only reason the village existed. The road and rail connections were developed for the coal but later allowed people to work in the village and commute to the major conurbations to the south.

We decided to perform a third run with the crystal on a larger-scale map. The map was smoothed onto the desks and the tripod positioned so it would have to travel in a direction that took it across or perpendicular to the valleys if it were to arrive at the same destination. We sat holding hands as we concentrated on Christine Olivetti and channelled our energies into making the pendant swing. Once the pendant was clearly moving the tripod, we broke our coven and made the coffee.

Megan asked after her mam and I assured her that Susan was in good form. She was uncomfortable from the operation and her surgeon had arranged for her to see his colleague in Newport General Hospital on Monday. Megan said she would phone and see if she needed company for the trip.

After lunch, the tripod had come to a stop and we saw that it was centred above the old mine buildings in the village of Blaengarw. We called Dave Williams and explained our findings. He said he would look into access and who would be able to guide us through the buildings. It turned out that the keys were lodged with the district council in Bridgend and one of the quantity surveyors was nominally in charge of the mine. The Coal Board carried out an annual inspection of the mine and to-date had used an ex-miner named Merion Llewellyn as guide. We felt we had done enough for the week, and as it was close to school out time, we called it a day. I picked up a copy of the Western Mail and walked to the Conservative club

Susan and I had a quiet weekend, which included a gentle walk in the Brecon Beacons prior to lunch at our favourite pub in Gilwern. Monday morning could not have come any sooner for me. I dropped Susan at home and was in the office at seven-thirty. Gwyneth had put a folder together with all the information we needed to search the Blaengarw mine. Dave walked in at eight o'clock. I made coffee and we sat at the map table looking at the tripod and pendant. Dave would not be able to accompany us to the mine but he was adamant that we should take two bobbies for protection. The two selected bobbies, Arthur and James, were not the type to sit around and twiddle their thumbs. They took our equipment list and had packed it neatly in the acquired Transit by the time the ladies arrived at nine-fifteen. I collected the keys from the surveyor at Bridgend which he gave up only on production of a copy of the court order. Megan collected Marion Llewelyn from his home in Betws and we all met up outside the mine entrance. In my hand, I had fifteen keys which were an access-all-areas ticket to the mine. In the folder, Gwyneth had drafted a key register, and as Marion selected a key and opened the padlock on the main gate, Gwyneth annotated the register with a key number and a description, that is, KEY 1 YALE 3 lever. Padlock. Main gate.

The lock parted easily but the metal hasp required more persuasion to move it. Marion was obviously prepared as a large GS screwdriver appeared in his hand as if by magic. The gate refused to move and Marion quickly directed me to position my Land Rover against a rubber-lined bracket that looked designed for the job. Slowly, the Land Rover overcame the rust of the past year and the gate screamed along the unlubricated rails. The mine could be divided in many ways but we chose to do clean and dirty. The clean would include admin, management, canteen, logistics, school. The dirty would include shower block, lamp room, locker room, electrical workshop, mechanical workshops, winding room, cage area and spoil handling area. We also had a key to the side gate.

We chose the clean area first. The canteen was mainly an open hall with a large stainless-steel counter down one side and the commercial kitchen equipment beyond the counter. Most of the equipment had been removed. There was no power, and even with the high-level windows, there was insufficient light to see into all the cupboards and passageways. As we left the canteen, Megan stopped and turned slowly in a circle, her face was contorted and her hands were raised to protect her ears. Marion locked the canteen as Megan came over to us and said,

"I hear them."

After drawing floodlight torches from the equipment van, we cleared the other clean areas without incident. The dirty areas were cleared more slowly; all six of us kept close together each with a very powerful torch. The shower block was clean, but with very few windows, the rooms and lockers were in darkness. The torches accentuated any items in the foreground and deepened the shadows in the background. The torches moving gave life to the shadows, causing several of us to pull up short whilst uttering expletives. I was happy to leave the shower block. The locker room was similar but had many more lockers in rows-upon-rows. We got used to the torch effect and cleared the rooms quickly. The route from the locker room was across an open-tarmacked area to the rooms below the large wheels which spun to lift the coal drams from the mine and to lower the workers into the depths. As we entered the lamp room, we saw the tallies that were allocated to each man. One of the two was given over for a lamp and battery whilst the second tally was given to the lift operator, or banksman, as you entered the cage. In this way, a record was kept of everyone who was down and provided a check that everyone had come up at the end of each shift. The lamp room and the lift shaft area were easy to clear but we did pay some attention to the actual shaft. The shaft was fairly securely closed but not airtight to allow a flow through the mine to reduce the build-up of any explosive gasses. The electrical workshop was a large barn-like building separated into two areas; a storage area where machinery was brought for repair and the materials needed for the repairs. The slightly smaller area was where the repairs were carried out and the tools and drawings were stored. The electrical workshop was a large building with many nooks and crannies and took some time to clear. The mechanical workshop was the largest building on the mine's estate; another barn like structure. In the floor, were several rail tracks, and overhead, was a gantry crane for handling the larger and heavier items. Concrete areas had been laid for the cleaner items to be repaired and serviced but other areas were compacted earth. The high-up windows like those in the other barn-like workshops were covered in years of grime which prevented most of the daylight from reaching the floor and the workshops built down each side of the barn. Megan, the two policemen and I searched every inch of the workshop. Gwyneth had resorted to her divining rods and paced slowly up and down the shed. We found nothing. Finally, we searched the winding room and the spoil handling area. Once again, the divining rods were used but no indication was received. We walked the areas beyond the active mine buildings right up to the side gate. We checked the key in the padlock; it worked. Megan had been keeping the key register up-to-date, and as we had now searched the mine, I asked if we had used all fifteen keys.

Megan replied, "We have used fourteen; there is one padlock missing." The time was getting on, and even though the ladies had arranged child-minding in the shape of Susan, it was rapidly getting to the end of the day. We slowly made our way back to the main gate. Gwyneth dowsing all the open areas as we walked back. At the gate, Marion closed the gate without any great effort and Arthur and James recovered our borrowed kit and carried out an inventory check before they departed. I made sure I had the mine keys as we walked to my car. Gwyneth stopped and cupped her hands to her ears. After several seconds, I too heard the call from a group of girls screaming for us to stop. We looked at each other and we both knew we had to return to the mine.

The drive back was strange; we were torn about the screams we had heard and Megan had heard similar alerts earlier in the day. We would discuss our failures and the missing padlock tomorrow.

## Chapter 10

WE assembled in the office by nine-fifteen and the atmosphere was strange, to say the least. Arthur and James were enjoying their out of the usual deployment. The ladies and myself were confused at the screams we had heard and the inability to identify the remaining padlock/keyhole. Dave Williams came in shortly after nine-thirty and we immediately briefed him on our failure of the previous day. Dave waited as we collected coffees and then we began a general discussion.

He listened carefully and then said, "It sounds as though you need to go back to the mine. You have James and Arthur for another day and you need to ascertain where key fifteen fits. Dave left and Arthur asked what kit we needed. After a short time to think, we came up with torches and shovels and something to remove padlocks, large padlocks. The ladies and I KNEW we had missed something but did not know what or how we had missed it. The key was, in fact, the key; we just had to find where and how it fitted.

I phoned the surveyor and quizzed him on his last inspection and the key number fifteen. He was very reticent to talk to me. I pushed the safety angle, saying no one would sign for an inspection he had not carried out, would he? He asked if we could meet for coffee, I agreed; he could not speak openly in the office. By eleven a.m., I was sitting opposite a young and inexperienced surveyor. He admitted that the inspection of the mine had not filled him with joy and the surveyor he took over from had talked him through the inspection and how to fill in the paperwork without setting foot in the mine. He was sure the man he replaced had never been there. Pulling a small wire bound notebook from his pocket, he fingered through the pages. He stopped at a list of keys. Key number FIFTEEN was listed as the ventilation shaft cabin built into the hill to the north of the mine site. He looked very sheepish, and as I explained what we were looking for, he realised that he could be in trouble. I told him that, if we were successful in our search, the inspection may get overlooked. We shook hands and I left.

By one-fifteen p.m., the ladies had returned, and I quickly brought them up to speed. We were sure we had heard their cries and this ventilation shaft cabin could be the missing area. Marion Llewelyn agreed to guide us to the ventilation shaft cabin and would meet us at the main gate at two-thirty p.m. James and Arthur checked our equipment list and asked if anything else was needed. Satisfied that all was in order, we set off in two vehicles; James and Arthur in the Transit and Megan, Gwyneth and I in the Land Rover.

Marion was waiting as we drew up at the front gate; his motorbike a superb-looking BSA Bantam, which we were told was his pride and joy, was parked to one side. He took the keys and opened the front gate. The gate moved much easier and without the infernal screeching of the previous day. Strangely, Gwyneth had her hands to her ears as if protecting them. She looked towards me and nodded, 'yes, I hear them.' We drove the vehicles inside and Marion pushed his Bantam inside. We pushed the gates too but did not lock them.

Marion jumped into the Transit and led us through the mine estate to the back or northern gate. He quickly opened the gate and jumped back into the Transit. The road from the gate was, at first, tarmac and then gave way to a gravel track. The road rose steeply from immediately outside the gate and made several switchbacks before arriving at a nondescript brick-built shed about twenty foot square with a green-painted wooden double door and a chimney cowl. There were no windows and the other discernible feature was slots left in the brickwork at a high level. This, we would later learn, was to help with the ventilation. Marion took the keys and approached the doors. The padlock seemed more modern than the building. Key number fifteen was selected, and although it was the same make as and easily entered the padlock, it would not turn. We tried all the compatible keys with no luck. It was a problem or a clue that could be investigated later, but for now, the bolt croppers would allow us access. Arthur handled the croppers like a pro. And with a loud crack and a tinkle, the padlock was on the floor. I asked them to bag it as someone other than the authorised key holder had replaced the lock. James, becoming the policeman of rank at the scene, donned plastic gloves and bagged the padlock. He also ensured he was first in the door and then turned and warned us not to contaminate the scene. The inside of the building, at first sight, looked to be completely empty. The main feature in the centre of the room was a sheet metal structure shaped like an inverted funnel. The wide part of the funnel was bolted to the floor and the narrow end formed a chimney which was connected to the cowl. Where the chimney flared to the floor, the circular structure was constructed of wedge-shaped pieces of pie with raised flanges which allowed it to be bolted together. Each steel pie also had an eyebolt fitted to allow it to be lifted. Several of the bolts in the two sections closest to the door were missing and most of the others were only finger-tight. Looking up above the sections of sheet metal pie, it was evident that hooks had been built into the roof to enable the sheet metal sections to be removed using a block and tackle. In the far corner of the building, concealed in the dark until our eyes adjusted, was a tool chest which contained the block and tackle. Within minutes, we had rigged the block and tackle and taken the weight of the cheese closest to the door. We slowly removed the rest of the bolts and raised the steel section. Once we manoeuvred the steel section out of the way, we recovered the torches from the police Transit and looked over the edge of the abyss. About sixty feet down was a circular shelf blocking most of the ventilation shaft. The remaining hole in the centre of the shaft was no more than five feet in diameter. The concrete was a much lighter in colour than the central shaft darkness and would have stood out on its own. However, the most striking feature of the scene was the black plastic rubbish sacks positioned around the circumference of the shelf every thirty degrees, like the hour marks on a clock. A quick count showed ten plastic bags. We phoned Dave Williams, and after a few minutes, the plan was formed. We would secure the site, James had padlocks within the Transit which could be used. Marion would be sworn to secrecy or locked up for the night; he chose to stay quiet. We would return to the station and plan for the recovery to be carried out tomorrow.

The next day, we met in the briefing room. Ian Forbes was the ranking officer and gave a speech with introductions and thanked each and every one for their efforts. He then handed it over to me. We used the screen and projector and talked everyone through the scene, employing some very competent photos taken by Arthur. It soon became evident that professional rescue personnel needed to be involved. Forensic scientists would need to be assisted in descending to the site. The recovery of bodies, if that is what they were, would only be started once the scene was cleansed. The meeting was adjourned to allow the teams from the Fire, Search and Rescue Service to be invited.

After lunch, we were called back to the briefing room and introduced to Station Officer Stuart Dixon. Stuart was the leader of the Brecon Beacons Search and Rescue

Team. He was the only paid team leader in the UK. He was about five-feet-nine of compact energy. He seemed to bounce as he walked and his Marine Commando Training had seen him operate in many of the world's hot spots, normally behind enemy lines. After the Marines, he became a solo mountaineer, climbing the world's most notorious pitches solo without rope support. He then settled down to rescuing people from all manner of situations and was soon offered the job of finding and rescuing people from the Beacons. Many were military personnel undergoing commando training.

We repeated the briefing from the morning to bring Stuart up to speed. As I finished, he stood without invitation, and quickly grasping the problems, outlined his plan and a list of kit that he would need. Ian Forbes asked if the kit was available and Stuart said his team were packing it as we speak and would drive to the site to arrive at nine a.m. tomorrow. Thursday was going to be a busy day. The ladies would meet us after the school run. Dave and I were on our way to our usual watering hole and we collected Stuart from the canteen on the way. We stayed a little too long and Dave gave us both a lift to the hotel. Stuart made his excuses and said he would meet us for dinner at eight. I ordered a pint and sat at my favourite table overlooking the lake. Susan answered after two rings and agreed to drive over for dinner. Finishing my drink, I went up to my room and brewed some coffee. I showered, and wrapped in a towel, took my coffee out onto the deck. Dinner was a strange two-hour period. Stuart and I were preoccupied with the details of the recovery, and though we tried to keep Susan up-to-date, she soon looked completely bored, and just after ten, took her leave and went home. Stuart was a complete professional and went to his room about ten-forty-five. The next day we met at the police station in the office allocated to the ladies and me. Dave Williams led the briefing. He started by saying that the mine was being searched again. Both gates were now manned by policemen and the ventilation shaft building had been opened up to allow the rescue team and the forensic team access. He apologised to me and the ladies and said access would be restricted until the forensic team had cleared the building and then the ventilation shaft. Because of the lack of parking at the subject building, only the rescue team vehicle and the forensic team van would be allowed beyond the gate. A police Land Rover would ferry any other equipment and personnel to the ventilation shaft building as required. This would not be until the top side part of the building was forensically cleared. I asked if we could be present during the recovery of the bodies if that is what they turned out to be. Dave agreed we had more right than anyone, to be present. Gwyneth and Megan stood and asked if they would be needed as they would feel better looking after their children. Dave accepted my nod as affirmative and agreed to the ladies standing down. They came over and said they would rather not be stood around doing nothing all day. I promised to keep them up-to-date. We drove in convoy to the mine and were signed into the main gate. In the canteen, a few tables had been assembled and two forensic technicians took our finger-prints and a saliva sample for DNA. We were issued with white Tyvek suits and plastic gloves and overshoes. The initial rescue team and three forensic technicians drove out of the north gate and up to the ventilation building. The forensic teams cleared the car park, the double doors and the area around the metal inverted funnel. Then they cleared the two segments of steel that had been interfered with. Stuart's rescue team rigged their own block and tackle attached to their Land Rover's winch and quickly and carefully removed the segments to the far side of the building where the forensic techs completed their examination. The rescue team rigged arc lights above the openings and illuminated the ventilation shaft. The block and tackle now became the descent apparatus. Stuart, in Tyvek and plastic gloves, donned a full-lift harness with a large steel ring between his shoulder blades. A thick elastic rubber wound shock absorber about two feet in length was permanently attached to the steel ring and ended in a D-shaped carabineer. The carabineer was slipped into the spring-loaded hook on the end of the steel winch cable. This allowed the wearer to detach himself at the bottom of the descent if necessary. A Mammut-type climbing rope was also attached to the steel ring and would remain connected as a safety rope. Stuart donned a full-face safety helmet with a large white-light lamp attached. The harness carried comms to his earpiece and a boom microphone on his left cheek. A knife was sheathed on his right thigh and a small axe was at his waist. On his left breast, was a carbon monoxide monitor and a small oxygen cylinder was on the right breast strap of his harness. A comms check was carried out. Before anything else was done, the rescue team received a briefing from the forensic team. Commonly called a 'don't' brief. It goes; don't touch anything, don't disturb anything, if you have to move anything, photograph it first. Stuart asked who would be next down and one of the Tyvek-suited bodies came forward. Stuart said he would need maybe five minutes on the lower floor, and as soon as he was down, his team would lower any kit the forensics needed and then the first tech. Everyone nodded. Stuart jumped onto the edge of the metal structure and spoke into the microphone, "take the weight." The winch revolved and lifted Stuart over the edge. Once he was happy that the harness was hanging him vertically, he called, "lower away!" As the winch started to lower, he called, "sixty!" The winch continued to lower, "thirty, twenty, ten!" The winch slowed, "three!" The winch almost stopped, "contact!" The winch stopped. He was on the ledge sixty feet down with only ten bodies for company.

Stuart tested the ground and asked for permission to unclip. The operations manager asked as to the visible dangers, especially the centre opening to the vent shaft. Stuart replied, "steel grid, strong enough for a man's weight." Manager asked, "monoxide monitor?" Stuart replied, "silent."

"Clear to unclip. Check safety rope."

Stuart, "Safety rope secure, unclipping." The helmet-mounted camera showed Stuart move to the first bundle. His gloved hand moved slowly over the black plastic bag. "Feels like human remains." Almost before the words registered top-side, Stuart slit the bag over the head of the remains. The familiar layers parted and the mummified face of a young girl was revealed. The lack of moisture in the ventilation shaft and the warm air coming up out of the mine had shrunken the flesh of the face, showing enlarged eye sockets containing very opaque eyes. The cheeks and lips were shrunken, pulling the mouth into a sinister grin and revealing her shiny white teeth. Stuart stepped back and reported one confirmed body of a young girl. He quickly walked to each bundle, and with a minimum of fuss, reported each as suspected human remains.

The winch retracted, and a few minutes later, the first pieces of forensic equipment landed on the ventilation shaft ledge. Stuart secured each item and returned the winch to the top. Two more trips and then the first forensic tech. One hour after the winch had dropped Stuart onto the ledge, all ten bundles had been checked and confirmed to hold human remains. Stuart called for two litters to be lowered. The litters were military stretchers with built-in straps that could be used to secure injured parties or, as in this case, bodies during rescue. The stretchers had four steel lift points to which a four-legged sling could be attached and connected to the winch by a centre ring. The forensic techs, having cleared each bundle, placed the first into the litter and it was lifted to the surface. By the time the litter returned, the second bundle was ready to be lifted, and by swapping the litters, the process of lifting all eleven bodies was over in ninety minutes. Within two hours, Stuart was clipping himself onto the steel cable, and with a long look around, he said, "ready to lift," and the manager replied, "winching." The bodies had been loaded into a black panel van and we watched as it moved very slowly down the dirt and gravel path toward the north gate. We were informed the bodies would be taken to four different sites for autopsy to try to get the reports as soon as possible. Stuart and his team replaced the steel segments and bolted them in place. They then packed their gear with practised familiarity. Just before four o'clock, they drove down to the north gate and parked up. Stuart then recorded his statement in the presence of a police officer and signed the tapes. Everyone came to wish him and his team goodbye and they drove away. I asked Dave if he needed me and he said, no. He would get a lift back and meet me in the Conservative Club at six. The hour's drive seemed to fly by.

I phoned Susan on the way back and she was in the Conservative club sitting with Harry Blackmore. He got up and shook my hand, "well done." He brought me a pint, and as we sat down, he asked, "can I tape this?" I agreed and warned Susan not to say anything. He questioned me as to what and where and who. I brought him right up to date.

Just before he finished the recording, he asked, "That makes twenty-nine. Is that you finished with the angels?" I thought for some time and then answered,

"I think so. The police will not want us involved in a manhunt which is, after all, their forté. The budget for our involvement will be pulled as soon as possible and I cannot think of any way they would want us involved if they found his lair and needed to give him an early morning call." Harry nodded, stopped his recorder and refilled our glasses. He pulled a small notebook from his pocket and flipped to a page with some large figures across the middle. This is the amount we think is due to you, if those bodies prove to be the remaining Angels of the Valleys. The figure was £230,000. He said his editor would confirm the figures once the remaining angels were identified and the account would then be settled. It was my turn to refill the glasses.

Harry then asked, "What about you two, you seem pretty sweet on each other?" Taking Susan's hand, I replied,

"We are good friends and I am having a house built close to the hotel overlooking the lake." Harry got up to leave and Dave sat down. He was beaming. "Come on, why are you so happy?"

"Derek, I have just been called into Lionel's office and been promoted." I could not have been happier and told him so. "The downside, is my last job as a Detective Sergeant is to give you and the ladies the sack." I told him I had just had this conversation with Harry so we knew it was coming. It transpired that we had a week's notice and the official notice would not be served until Monday, so we would be expected to be out of our office by cease-of-play Friday. We were all in very good moods, and after a further pint, Dave asked if we could join him and Elaine for dinner. He suggested a place that was new to me but Susan gave it a good report.

The Green Fern was on the outskirts of Brynithel and was arranged with tables in islands off a central kitchen and bar. With three tables in each island room, each table had a wonderful view over the valley towards Aberbeeg and Six Bells. The view during the day was good, but as the darkness descended and the lights started to twinkle, it was somewhere special. The food was good and the company, as always, was excellent. A pianist played for tips and took on any song requested, the length of the performance dictated by the size of the donation. The small dance floor between the piano and bar gave the place a very intimate feel but did little to hide my poor dancing. Slightly the worse for wear, we climbed into separate taxis and Susan and I were soon sitting on the deck overlooking the lake outside my hotel room. Susan spoiled the mood somewhat with the announcement that she had an appointment at Addenbrookes Hospital in two weeks' time. I was scared but she explained it was only a routine examination as it had been three months since the operation. How the time had flown…

Monday morning was difficult. We had affected a lot of people, both in the station and around the area, and a lot of them had read Harry's final pieces in the Sunday paper. Our office was like a party venue, with people dropping in to express their good wishes and congratulate us on our successes. At about eleven a.m., Lionel came in. He hugged everyone and wished us all the best for the future. As he finished his coffee, he pulled me to one side and asked if I could attend a briefing on Thursday in Cowbridge. I agreed and he added, "we should have the identities of the eleven by then." I was about to shake his hand when he said, "don't pack the office up. I've arranged a stay of execution for your team. It's only a week but it takes you to the end of the month; easier for the money people." I shook his hand, and as he left, I found the girls and told them of the extension to our contract. That afternoon, Dave called for a briefing, and at one-thirty, we gathered in our office. Around the table were the three of us; Dave acting as chairman, several detective sergeants, two detective constables and Harry Blackmore. Dave certainly knew how to deliver a surprise. Harry was almost persona-non-grata with the police. Dave opened the meeting, explaining that the people around the table were the ones closest to the case. Harry had faithfully recorded each disappearance and was the only one who persistently warned of a serial killer. The psychics—our group—had found the four burial sites which provided most of the forensic evidence. The serving policemen at the table had followed up on the evidence and may have come closest to identifying the killer. Dave gave me the floor and I explained how we came to be involved, how we traced the sites using the residual energies of the victims and how we confirmed the nature of the sites before turning the delicate work of recovery and identification to the relevant authorities. Detective Sergeant Rob Morris spoke for the police. He told how they had followed up on a lot of the leads and theories that my team had come up with. The types of vehicles, type of buildings needed, the farms that were not producing anything and/or running any stock. They also took on the forensic examination of the tape, which was still yielding glimmers of evidence, but not much. As the conversation slowed to a crawl, Harry turned to Gwyneth and asked rather pointedly,

"Gwyneth, have you anything to add?" Gwyneth looked a little sheepish as she replied,

"When I was between sixth form and college, I worked for an animal feed supplier, Pattisons. We took the orders to the outlaying farms, usually delivering directly to the inside of barns and storage sheds. On that tape, I saw a reflection of an unusual window that rang a bell but I cannot remember where I saw it."

Dave was the first to ask, "Are you sure it was in the film?"

"Yes I watched it several times and the window is totally out of place." Dave then asked if anyone else had anything to add. Officially closing the meeting, he asked everyone to remain seated. When we all had coffees in front of us, he said,

"Anything to be added that didn't need to be recorded."

One of the detective sergeants said, "What if he strikes again, when is he due to strike again?" Dave deflected the question to me.

I answered, "The killer is a creature of habit and should strike in six to eight weeks' time."

A detective sergeant by the name of Steve asked, "How long would you be involved?" I replied that we had jobs until the end of the month but were willing to assist, if allowed, until the killer was caught. Dave thanked everyone for their time. He then asked Rob Morries to look into the window evidence. As the meeting broke up, Gwyneth sought out Harry and asked him how he remembered her bit with the windows. He said he was going through the taped interviews and came across the sentence about the windows and he realised it could be important. Harry then asked her how many places she delivered to. She answered about seven a day so forty to forty-five a week. Rob Morris asked if Pattisons were still in business. Harry said they were but now operated from Newport. As the office emptied, the ladies took their leave to collect the kids from school, leaving Dave and me sitting in the easy-chairs.

Dave spoke first, "We are bloody close! If we identify those windows from aerial photos or estate agent's sale blurb, we will have him." I suggested the Conservative club and Dave agreed but he needed a few minutes. I walked slowly to the club whilst Dave phoned Lionel and requested armed response be placed on twenty-four hour standby. We sat close to the door and drank in silence. I was just going to refill our drinks when Dave held up his hand and said,

"No more, I need to stay completely sober in case we find that farm tonight." I returned to the hotel, and taking my lead from Dave, I brewed a pot of coffee. I phoned Susan and brought her up to date on the case. I invited her for dinner but she declined, saying she was going to Megan's to eat with the grandchildren. We agreed to meet for dinner tomorrow. I had several pieces of administration to complete and was tucked up in bed before ten.

The next morning was quiet with very little happening in the station. Dave, as operational ranking officer, was at the local police firearms range, requalifying to carry a standard issue sidearm. All operational ranking officers were encouraged to keep their skills up to a required standard. The number of times ranking officers were issued firearms was reducing every year as the armed response teams took more and more responsibility for the security of operational deployments. Gwyneth had made several enquiries with old friends on which farms they delivered to and whether they remembered the windows that looked out of place.

Just before ten o'clock, a young man came in and asked for Gwyneth. They chatted for several minutes and then Gwyneth pinned a photo on the board. It showed a bleak hillside view with a farmhouse in the foreground. The barn was not huge but the distinct windows at high-level made it stand out. The windows were about three feet wide and five feet high but it was not the dimensions that made them stand out, it was the arched tops—much too expensive and flamboyant for a normal farm building. Gwyneth walked to the large wall map, and picking up a large red flag that was completely out of scale with the map, she carefully positioned the flag to indicate the target farm. We held our collective breath as she picked up the red marker pen and wrote neatly, "Manmoel, Owl Reach Farm."

The room descended into silence. Everyone needed to be doing something but it seemed nobody knew what to do or how. Ian came to our rescue and issued several short orders to individuals. A really large-scale map of the area surrounding the farm was acquired and laid out on the large table. The tiny road out of Manmoel terminated two hundred yards after passing the gates of a farm. The road then became a sheep path unsuitable for most vehicles. Details of the farm, the owner, the number of family members, registered motor vehicles and amount of animals and crops produced were quickly complied. Dave arrived just as Ian finished briefing the police helicopter, crew call sign nine-nine. He asked them to film the road from Manmoel north to an area about one mile north of the farm. By three o'clock, we were gathered around a large screen onto which was a projection of helicopter nine-nine's reconnaissance flight. The helicopter hovered briefly over the outskirts of Manmoel then turned north and followed a small single-track road higher into the hills. Some passing places had been provided, but the centre of the road quickly turned to grass which was an indication of the lack of traffic along this road. The helicopter held clear of the farm but the windows in the barn were clear for all to see. Swinging around, the helicopter passed to the west of the farm and followed the track for approximately one mile. The ground was barren and the track was reduced to two ruts historically walked by sheep and followed by sheep farmers on motorbikes, and more lately, on four-by-four quad bikes. Chris Mason arrived; he had been tasked with finding background on the farm. He wasted no time in getting down to the facts and handed out a precis of his brief as he spoke, The farm was owned by a husband and wife, Martin and Bethany. They owned a Land Rover, a Ducato van, a Cortina estate and a Husqvarna scrambler-type motorcycle. Martin, white, was of German origin, the son of Julian Weis who escaped Nazi Germany on the kinder transport and settled in South Wales after a period in the Bridgend POW camp. There was a general hubbub in the office, as individual officers remembered stories about the pair and wondered if Bethany knew anything about the killings. We were feeling a little left out, and as lunchtime approached, the ladies left to do the school run. I walked slowly to the Conservative club and ordered a pint. As I sat down, I was surprised and delighted to see Ian Forbes enter the bar. He collected his drink, vodka and tonic, and joined me at a back table away from prying eyes and large ears. He raised the drink in salute and offered the comment, "Briefing the boss at two." I explained I felt like a spare member at an orgy. Our job appeared to be over and we wouldn't be in at the kill, so to speak. He then surprised me by saying he was here to invite the three of us to the briefings this afternoon and the operation briefing at four o'clock tomorrow morning. He had also secured a place for me with his team in the control vehicle if I was interested. His vehicle would have only a watching brief as Dave Williams would be Officer-in-Charge but we would have access to all comms and be privy to the decisions in real-time. I was over the moon!

We were back in the briefing room by one-thirty p.m. There was a large number of people already seated and the ladies and myself chose seats at the back just as Lionel stepped to the lectern.

"Derek, please bring your team to the front." Shyly, we shuffled to the front row. Our embarrassment was eased by Dave who stood and showed the ladies to their seats. Lionel was very generous in his praise of our efforts in locating the bodies of the Angels of the Valleys. After a quick overview of the coming operation, Lionel handed over to Dave Williams. The police had decided that this was a dangerous operation. Each of the different police sections was introduced and their part in the coming operation was explained:

Firearms unit—provide protection for all others and provide the initial "knock squad." They would also provide an ambush team for the path to the north of the farm.

Forensic team—to carry out the initial search and protect all evidence.

Police site and evidence team—to control and preserve the site and ensure the chain of evidence rules are followed.

Arrest and custody team—to take suspects into custody, ensure they know their rights and remove them to detention in an expeditious manner.

Medical team—A ambulance manned with two paramedics.

Helicopter on standby with doctor and paramedic.

Control vehicles—every man on the ground would have a police radio.

Fire engine—just in case.

Dave then outlined the plan of action for the morning.

The ambush team, comprising three armed officers, would find a position to the north of the farm and stop anyone escaping from the primary site, that is the farmhouse.

Four armed officers would cover the immediate area around the farmhouse.

Three armed officers plus the key man would force entry at the front door. No warning would be issued other than, "armed police officers," once the door was breached.

The ranking officer, Dave Williams, would travel in the armed response control vehicle. He would defer to the Armed Response Team leader until the breach and capture phase was complete.

Ian Forbes (and me) would wait outside the farm perimeter and maintain an overall watching brief by video until the active phase of the operation was complete.

When the armed squads reported, "in position," the key man and three armed officers would breach the front door. Two officers would ascend the stairs and make the arrests. The key man, having discarded the big red key, would assist the third armed officer in clearing the downstairs rooms of the farmhouse. Two minutes after the knock, the four armed officers would move from their covering positions to assist in the farmhouse. If the suspects manage to escape the farmhouse, the ambush team would be ordered to stop them and the police helicopter would be launched to monitor their escape.

All personal radios would be switched to whisper mode and double-click on the talk button for an affirmative answer.

Dave finished off with a question-and-answer session and set the knock time as five-forty-five hours. From this time, each team leader worked out their own timeline to ensure they were in position before a quarter-to-six the next morning.

We were in the briefing room at four-fifteen hours. Ian Forbes and Dave Williams were standing in front of a whiteboard and Dave had already crossed off several units that had been contacted and were mobile or in position. Over the next ten minutes, Dave completed the checklist. Dave spoke briefly to Ian about operational control and who would assume control if certain scenarios were to develop. They shook hands and Dave left. Ian called me over and said, "time to go. First stop, the gents; could be a long morning."

The drive was only thirty minutes and then we climbed slowly up the mountain track toward Owl Tree Farm. The early morning mist was already receding up the hillside allowing us to turn out our lights. We kept the engine revs low to minimise noise and we reached our operational position just before 0500 hours. Radio messages were flashed to Dave confirming that the operational units were in position. We were too early; the next forty-five minutes would drag by. We listened in as Dave used his mobile to contact the secondary units; fire, ambulance, helicopter and forensics, all reported ready. Dave, knowing the chances for detection increased with each waiting minute, switched to personal radio and called, "All units standby. OPERATIONAL TIME CHANGE. KEY TEAM KNOCK NOW. KNOCK NOW. GO, GO, GO!

The four-man team moved swiftly across the yard. The three rifles covering the windows of the farmhouse. The fourth man carried a bright yellow weighted battering ram. He positioned the ram next to the lock and swung it back, accelerating it into the wooden door. The noise was deafening in the quiet morning air, the wood splintered but the door held! The key man swung the ram again and the door swung open. Two armed officers entered the house and started up the stairs. The third armed officer and the key man entered the house, shouting the required, "ARMED POLICE!" and started to clear the downstairs rooms. As the first two armed officers reached the top of the stairs, a woman appeared from one of the bedrooms and tried to block their paths. Disregarding the weapons, she flew at them and was lucky not to have been killed. They quickly subdued the woman but she had served her purpose. From the other bedroom, a two-stroke motor kicked into life and a motorcycle hurtled up a makeshift ramp and disappeared through a large picture window. The speed attained on the ramp allowed the rider to jump the short distance from the window to the hill at the back of the farmhouse. The rider landed the jump perfectly and the powerful motor hurled the machine up the hillside. The armed officer on that side of the house was unable to gain a clear shot, as the rider was now passing through a small valley, hiding him from the officers. Radio chatter started, "suspect on motorcycle heading north." Ambush team, "received." Dave called the helicopter and ordered it to get airborne.

The motorcycle sped up the cleared path to the north; the rider really hyped that he had escaped the ambush. His preparations had given him a chance to outwit the police, however, the fact that he was running meant the police knew of his crimes. The goggles he wore were clearing slowly but prevented him from spotting the three officers dug into camouflaged hides on either side of his path. The lead officer radioed, "suspect in sight, we have a shot." Without hesitation, Dave answered, "take the shot." The bullet smashed into the rider's chest, fragmenting as it hit the sternum, and tumbling and tearing through his lungs, trachea and heart. He was dead before his hand slipped around the throttle and slowed the bike. The bike and rider fell slowly onto its right side and proceeded to cartwheel across the hillside. The ambush team leader radioed, "target neutralised." Dave radioed, "open radios," and proceeded to bring the operation to a close. The ambush team were brought in and the kill weapon was cleared and impounded. All other weapons were cleared in an unloading area. Each armed officer filled in an operational statement and signed the bottom of the form. Dave signed the site over to the regular policemen and the forensic teams started the evidence collection that would prove vital in the coming trial. The helicopter did a slow pass over of the scene, confirmed they were stood down and disappeared south back to its base at Rhoose Airport. Bethany was placed in a police car and driven away. Her fate to be decided by the courts and highly-paid barristers.

Ian and Dave dropped me at the Conservative club, and from the conversation in the car on the way back, there was some friction between them, but overall, both were happy with the outcome of the morning's operation. Several police officers were in the club and the mood was fast approaching party central. I took a pint to a table toward the back of the room close to the fruit machines. Within five minutes, my phone rang and Harry Blackmore asked where I was. Ten minutes later, he placed a pint in front of me and sat down with his favourite Bell's. He asked about the operation and told him only what I thought I could, legally. Having wheedled enough out of me and presumed a whole lot more, Harry left to write his scoop. Before he left, he placed an envelope on the table and said, "final payment from the paper and insurance companies." The cheque brought the final total to £249,000. The ladies would be pleased. I certainly was!

I had only just started the pint that Harry brought when my phone rang. Susan had heard of the arrest and wondered where I was. I told her I was just waiting for Dave and Ian to come in. I invited her to join me and she accepted, saying she would be there in an hour. Ian Forbes walked in; he was dressed in full uniform and was smiling like the proverbial Cheshire cat. He signalled to me for a drink. I lifted my beer to indicate I was okay. He took my signal to mean, 'yes,' so, I again had two drinks before me. As he sat down, I noticed his rank insignia had gained an extra pip. I asked about his promotion and he explained that Lionel was waiting when they returned, and after a short debrief, he asked Ian to meet him in Chief Inspector's office. When Ian had walked into the office most of the detective division of Abertillery were there. Lionel made a short speech and presented Ian with new rank badges and the ceremonial keys to the office he already occupied. Ian was already the Chief Inspector Elect and had been doing the job for the past year. I asked after Dave and was told Lionel was at present briefing him on his new role as Abertillery's new Inspector and it would be a race to see which of them would be first to come through the door. Dave was first but only by a short head. Lionel was generous in the praise of everyone involved in the case and quick to spend his allowance over the bar. Susan arrived slightly later than planned and was immediately drawn into the party. The party slowly wound down and Susan offered to give me a lift to the hotel. I managed to say my goodbyes and we left. When we were sitting on the deck outside my room, overlooking the lake, Susan reminded me that she needed to be in Cambridge to see her oncologist at two o'clock tomorrow. We decided she would stay at the hotel for dinner and then go home so she could prepare for the hospital visit. We spent a very pleasant couple of hours eating and drinking, and around nine-thirty p.m., Susan left to get a good night's sleep. I did the calculations for the reward money and wrote cheques for Gwyneth and Megan. Each cheque was placed in an individual envelope and addressed to the girls. I dropped the envelopes at the bar and asked if they could be posted and the stamp costs be added to my bill.

After breakfast, I went to the police station and collected my personal kit. I left my police phone, radio and ID card on the desk. The Land Rover was low on fuel so I stopped at the garage and filled it to the brim. I returned to the hotel and dropped off my personal kit. I ordered a coffee and sat at a table outside the bar. Dave Williams, looking slightly the worse for wear, turned up unexpectedly. I ordered him coffee and he explained he had been to the police station and been told I had been in earlier. He wanted to see me before I left as he was unsure if I was returning to Norfolk or not. I told him that today I was taking Susan to hospital and we would be back about seven tonight. Thursday and Friday I would disentangle myself from Abertillery police and Susan and I would decide our future. I promised he would be the third to know my plans.

Susan was standing in the road talking to a neighbour when I turned up. I got out to load Susan's case into the back and was introduced to Alison Sims. She remembered my Uncle Ron and Aunty Dyllis, who previously lived on the same street, and their children Dianne, Meryl and Gerald.

We drove quietly, south to meet the M4 at Newport. I broached the subject of living in South Wales or Norfolk. Susan thought for a short while and then asked that I wait until after the hospital visit. We joined the M4 and I settled the Landie at just above the speed limit; always the renegade. The first sign of problems came as we approached the flat area to the west of the second crossing. The radio normally tuned to Radio 2 providing a strong clear signal, started to wander up and down the dial and squelched, and no amount of tuning could reduce the interference. Susan turned the radio off and loaded a CD into the slot of the CD player. The Eagles played the intro and the first line of Hotel California and then the interference resumed. Susan looked at me and turned the whole unit off; still the noise of interference was heard and increased in volume. As the bridge came into view, the far bank appeared to be covered in cloud which was definitely not in the forecast. As we came closer to the bridge, the cloud was more like a sandstorm, a solid three hundred feet high wall of blackness that obscured everything beyond its leading edge. Susan sat serenely, staring straight ahead with a slight smile playing along her lips. As we approached the middle of the main span of the bridge, the leading edge appeared to have advanced and was now climbing steadily up the roadway toward us. I slowed the Landie to give myself more thinking time. There were no other vehicles on the road. I put the lights on and selected main beam. No comment from Susan. The speed of approach of the leading edge was increasing. Still nothing could be seen inside the storm. The bonnet of the Land Rover disappeared into the blackness. Fascinated, I glanced sideways and Susan's lips moved to what I took to be a goodbye. All colour inside the car had turned to grey, and as the storm entered the car, my legs disappeared and everything else dissolved into pixels...

A familiar voice asked, "Jolene not to take her man." The owl spoke of rapid eye movement and reducing the drugs that kept me under. Sometime later, I opened my eyes to discover I was still in a Cambridge hospital where I had been since the accident some fourteen weeks earlier. After several days of tests and the ubiquitous bladder and bowel movement, I was cleared to go home. My daughter, Jo, arrived to take me home on Thursday. Before we left, I walked the wards and corridors listening for the singing hospital worker. Alas, I never found her. It's two-and-a-half hours from Cambridge to my house in Norfolk. We opened the door and I was surprised to not find a pile of letters on the doormat. Jo informed me the housekeeper she had employed at the recommendation of my neighbour was very good. So it proved; the house was very clean, my bed had clean sheets and every room was aired. We made coffee and sat in the conservatory. I put the phone on speaker and listened to friends and neighbours express their concerns for me and condolences for the loss of my wife. The last message made me spill my coffee. "THIS IS IAN FORBES OF THE ABERTILLERY POLICE…"

## THE END

# ANGELS THE FINAL LIST

| NAME | DATE MISSING | FOUND | BURIAL SITE |
|---|---|---|---|
| Claire Meredith | Aug. 2010 | YES | ABERTILLERY PARK |
| Linda Lewis | Dec. 2009 | YES | BLAENGARW |
| Christine Olivetti | Feb. 2009 | YES | BLAENGARW |
| Imogen Tyler | Dec. 2008 | YES | NEWBRIDGE |
| Margaret Groves | May 2007 | YES | BLAENGARW |
| June Thomas | Aug. 2006 | YES | CLYDACH RESERVOIR |
| Leslie James | Dec. 2005 | YES | NEWBRIDGE |
| Angela Moores | May 2005 | YES | ABERTILLERY PARK |
| Linda Lloyd | Sept. 2004 | YES | BLAENGARW |
| Margaret Hines | Dec. 2003 | YES | BLAENGARW |
| Rose Cassidy | Aug. 2002 | YES | CLYDACH RESERVOIR |
| Carol Williams | Dec. 2001 | YES | BLAENGARW |
| Barbara Amber | May 2000 | YES | NEWBRIDGE |
| Ruby Noble | Jan. 2000 | YES | ABERTILLERY PARK |
| Pamela Amphlett | May 1999 | YES | CLYDACH RESERVOIR |
| Sheila Audrey | Aug. 1998 | YES | BLAENGARW |
| Sandra Morgan | Dec. 1997 | YES | NEWBRIDGE |

| | | | |
|---|---|---|---|
| Denise Williams | May 1997 | YES | BLAENGARW |
| Lynne Green | Aug. 1996 | YES | CLYDACH RESERVOIR |
| Edith Jones | Jan. 1996 | YES | NEWBRIDGE |
| Laura Smith | May 1995 | YES | CLYDACH RESERVOIR |
| Alison English | Aug. 1994 | YES | BLAENGARW |
| Jemima Armstrong | Dec. 1993 | YES | CLYDACH RESERVOIR |
| Sarah Butcher | Jan. 1993 | YES | ABERTILLERY PARK |
| Anne Brightwell | May 1992 | YES | BLAENGARW |
| Chloe Featherstone | Aug. 1991 | YES | NEWBRIDGE |
| Paris Winters | Dec. 1990 | YES | NEWBRIDGE |
| Leonie Ford | May 1990 | YES | NEWBRIDGE |
| Judy Manchester | Aug 1989 | YES | CLYDACH RESERVOIR |